WHITE TRASH GOTHIC 2

EDWARD LEE

DEADITE PRESS
833 SE Main Street #342
Portland, OR 97214
www.DEADITEPRESS.com

AN ERASERHEAD PRESS COMPANY
www.ERASERHEADPRESS.com

ISBN: 9781621053248

Copyright © 2019 by Edward Lee
Cover art copyright © 2019 Jim Agpalza

All rights reserved. No part of this book may be reproduced or transmitted in any form or by any means, electronic or mechanical, including photocopying, recording, or by any information storage and retrieval system, without the written consent of the publisher, except where permitted by law.

ACKNOWLEDGMENTS

Frank and Inge Festa, Samia Salah, Ian Fischer, Bob Hinton, Christine Morgan, Dustin LaValley, Vivian Lamade, Sandy and Tony, Lorilee Perez, Jane Breslin, Erik P., Samantha Wood, Michael Schmidt, Christopher Newton, Tina Ayres, Amy Farmer, Victor Butler, Josh Myers, Elizabeth Macula, Bobby Kursavi for the "nipples" line, Steve Hergina, William Skaar, William Tea, Timothy Burnhill, Fabian Brunetti, Joey Trevino, Babaganoosh, Frank Arthur Hoshman, VeryEvilDead (who got a Bighead tattoo!), Becky Narron, Aggy DiTullio and John, Rainer, Joshua Slusser, Cleta Simonin, Tiffany Crystal Whitt, Marc Schnieder, Damian from Brisbane Australia, Sue Ely, Alexander Kogler, Shavonne Pagliughi, Dan Spelina, Markus Solty, Manuel Mitterlehner and Katharina, Anthony Vacca, Kayla Wilson, Shaun Booe, Josh McCaw, Justin Joseph, Brett Cotov, Anthony Vacca, Alex R., Ellie Gibbons, Erin Shaw, Stephen Pontius, Kylie, Anthony Polley, and all my great friends in Germany, and the wonderful people I met at Leipzig Bookfair: Dorian, Laura, Florian, Carlo, Andi, Patrick, Hardy, Anett, Yvi, David, Christian, Lisa Ille, and especially Arya Green and Candymandy, and Daniela Nicolaus who has an Edward Lee tattoo!

WHITE TRASH GOTHIC SAGA by EDWARD LEE:
White Trash Gothic
White Trash Gothic 2
White Trash Gothic 3

A WORD FROM THE AUTHOR

The word is this: Sorry! My friends, many of you have been supporting my career for decades, and for this, I am inexpressibly grateful. For the majority of those decades I've always managed to produce new horror fiction at a respectable pace; I'm quite happy with those productions, and I know that many or you are as well. Over the past few years, however (and I shudder to say it) I've become encumbered by this outrageous thing called Getting Older—an inevitable curse. What a ripoff! At any rate, I'm writing this note to convey my uttermost apologies for taking SO LONG to finish this relatively short book. My levels of physical and creative energy aren't what they used to be; hence, it takes me longer to complete each new project. All I can say, from the bottom of my heart, is thank you for your patience. I hope you enjoy reading Part Two of my White Trash Gothic saga as much as I enjoyed writing it. And there will indeed be a Part 3, and I can promise you it won't take me forever to write it. Thank you all for your devoted support!

Sincerely,
Ed Lee

WHITE TRASH GOTHIC 2

HOMECOMING

"Shee-it, fella," twanged the overalled white-trash old man behind the counter of the LUCKY'S LAST STOP MOUNTAIN SHOP. The crackly voice snapped further: "We don't sell gas, nor nothin' else, ta nigguz."

Whoa! thought the well-dressed black man opposite him. He smiled broadly. "Are you *serious?* In *this* day and age? Even in West Virginia hill country, that's a bit archaic, isn't it? *Nigguz?*"

The old man stared him down with sunken, hooded eyes bracketed by deep wrinkles. There was little doubt that one of the crabbed hands concealed by the counter grasped some sort of firearm. "Git'cher black porch-monkey ass off a my property, less'n you wanna be swingin' in the woods in a hour." Bad dentures showed through a sly grin. "Wouldn't be the first nigguh we'se strung up out there."

The black man's shoulders slumped his neat gray suit jacket. This was too preposterous; he couldn't even generate anger, and no vestige of his old self so much as blinked. He put a $20 bill on the counter. "Just, please, ring me up for twenty on pump three."

"I reckon bein' a smoke ain't'cher only problem," droned the old man. "Guess you gots a *hearin'* problem ta go along with that black skin." He called out. "Chester! We gots a uppity one out here."

A thunking was heard—footsteps on the wood floor—and in a moment "Chester" presented himself.

The black man thought of L'il Abner, only this guy was bigger. Six-ten at least, 300 pounds, at least. No fat, all muscle. The guy had to duck, and then he *squeezed* himself through the backroom doorway. Slicked back black hair, redneck flannel shirt, redneck canvas work pants, giant clod-hopper redneck boots. A peninsula-sized jaw. This goliath looked right at the black man and said, "Nigguh…"

"You got it, Chester. I'm a *nigguh*—" The black man gritted blazing white teeth as he seemed to search for something in his mind. "Chester *McCroy?* Or is it Mc*Kray?*"

"Dag it, Chester!" cracked the proprietor. "How the *fuck* does this spear-chucker know your name?"

"Nuh-nevuh seen him a'fore," Chester's baritone quavered a bit. His eyes squinted confusion. "Dun't know him…"

"That's right, Chester, you don't know me," the outsider agreed. "But I sure know you. Angel told me all about you."

At this remark, Chester's eyes went wide, and his lower lip began to tremble.

"Yeah, you know. Angel? Your little sister—"

"Dag blam it, Chester!" the old man barked. "How the hell this *nigger* know you had a sister!?"

"Right, sir," the black man said. "*Had.* Past tense. She died awhile back, huh, Chester? And you as good as killed her yourself—"

Chester, pink-faced now, rushed the black man, and lifted him three feet off the floor by his shoulders. "I did not kill her!" his voice boomed. "She disser-peered! Got abductered, the cops say!"

"Yes, but she didn't actually disappear, she ran away, right? At about fourteen? Who could blame the poor girl? Come on. Raped every day by you and your step-daddy. Hell, the *day she was born* was when you and step-dad started jerking off in her mouth, couple times a day, both of you, right? A new-born baby doesn't know what's going on—poor little kid practically *lived* on your sperm. What kind of sick hayseed pile of shit can do stuff like that? To a *baby?* And of course, once she got a little older, well, you and dad started dippin' your wicks big time, huh? Used her for your own private party. That stuff screwed her head up for good, never stood a chance, did she?

And by the time she was thirteen or fourteen, you and step-dad knocked her up. You told everyone it was the 'creekers.'" And then the black man let out a cynical laugh; he landed on his feet when the goliath released him.

The old man looked cock-eyed at Chester. "You really do all that dirty stuff, Chester?"

Chester wobbled in place, crying, shaking his head no.

"He sure did, pops, and he knows it." The black man loped to the reach-in and removed a can of Fanta grape soda. "Even *you'd* be surprised by how many little kids this big meat-rack has raped. It's enough to make the devil throw up." Then he raised the can of soda. "Oh, I'm helping myself. You don't mind, do you?"

Chester dropped to his knees, slouched over, blubbering away.

"Oh, look at him, he's a big baby now, a big blubbering sick in the head redneck *baby.*" The black man continued with his vision. "So Angel ran away, couldn't hack it any more, was half-nuts by then anyhow. Then she had the misfortune to get picked up hitchhiking by a group of really rough customers. Hell, those guys make you and your step-daddy look like a couple of Teletubbies and, well, it's best that I show you rather than tell you…"

The black man put his hand on Chester's head, and when he did so, Chester gasped.

"Take a look, Chester, take a good look at what those scumbags did to your innocent sister."

By now, the visions forced into Chester's head incapacitated him. He gagged, hacked, sobbed, and tremored, while the black man stood over him, looking down as if from a high bluff.

"But take heart, Chester. Angel is in Heaven now. When you die three years from now, you *won't* be joining her."

Chester had been rendered inert, a useless, blubbering mass of hillbilly muscle. Which left the old man, who now stood behind the counter, holding a shotgun. "I warned ya, nigguh. Ya got 'til three to leave, less'n ya want to leave feet first."

"Okay." The black man went along. "One, two, three. Don't make me laugh, *Lucky.* No shells in that shotgun. Your cheap cracker ass is too piss-poor to buy any." The black man smiled brightly as ever as the shotgun was dropped to the floor and the proprietor's face lengthened and blanched.

"See, you picked the wrong *nigguh* to shit on today. You picked a *psychic* nigguh. Now, *please.* Ring me up for twenty on pump three." The black man half-left, stopped, then put his head back in. "Oh, you're gonna die about sundown next Tuesday or Wednesday—I'm not sure which. A dude's gonna walk in here, put a gun to your head, and then kill ya because there'll only be six bucks in the drawer." Again, the black man half-left, recollected himself, and put his head back in. "Oh, and it's gonna be a *white* guy, not a *nigguh.*"

Now the black man made his full departure from the premises, chuckling under his breath. *Damn, I'm really on the mark tonight...*

Off he went then, after filling the tank, leaving the squalid gas station and store behind. The heart of Virginia was like his old life in a sense: far behind him now. The sun setting behind the Allegheny Mountains looked surreal and beatific. Darkness poured quickly into the valley, summoning still more gorgeous imagery. Times like these were what brought the black man to his most resplendent moments of peace and faith...

Yes. Back behind the wheel of the Rectory's old Mercedes, tires humming, winding ribbons of asphalt conjuring him onward. He took a last look at the sunset before it vanished, and with that vanishing, all the awfulness and human horror in the world vanished too. Only beauty remained—unfathomable beauty, unpronounceable, and bereft of error. The black man needed no further proof than this to know that God existed and was with him. This reflection, of course, was all very transcendental and lyric but he liked this little ornament for the day. He'd seen *much more* proof of God in the last decade, enough to make Caiaphas and all the Pharisees bow down to Jesus and offer their heads.

He'd already passed Pulaski, Christiansburg, and Radford—which were among many of his former stomping grounds. Exit Virginia, enter *West* Virginia. *Another world,* thought the black man, sipping his grape soda. No main highways or state routes would take him to his destination, thanks to the obstacle of the Alleghenies. From here on it was just rising and falling byways and mountain roads wending through the hills, many of such originating centuries ago as Indian trails, trails first used for trading with other tribes before their re-utilization as war-paths. *No grape soda back then, no sir. No Starbucks, no wi-fi, no nothin'...* The black man enjoyed some of the names: Chief Cornstalk Road, Greasy Ridge Road, Scriller's Ghost Road, and, yes, even Hog Ball Road. Diamond-shaped yellow signs let one know this was Redneck Land: FALLING ROCKS, DEER CROSSING, SLIPPERY WHEN WET, etc., all pitted by the traditional double-ought buck.

So he drove on, and even though the GPS navigator wouldn't work out here, he doubted it would be long before he arrived at his destination.

The black man's name, by the way, was Tyrone Grant, though for all of his adult life he'd been known by his "street" name, which was "Case Piece." This, since he'd experienced his transfiguration, he'd changed to "Case *Peace*."

His current destination was Luntville, West Virginia.

***

You've GOT to be kidding me, groaned the Writer at the crack of noon the next day when he finally managed to leave the hotel. The blaze of sun "smote" him like a blow, and this smite was not appreciated by the Writer's hangover. *One too many Collier's Civil War Lagers,* he regretted. He reached for his sunglasses but realized then that he'd never owned a pair in his life.

He'd risen at ten, showered, then managed to do some laundry after an expenditure of time that could only be defined as *undue. I'm old, lazy and, well, an alcoholic—big deal?* he tried to rationalize.

Portafoy had guided him to the hotel's guest laundry, and had even offered to wash and dry the Writer's clothes because, "You seem, if you'll pardon my saying it, sir, not to have benefited much from your night's sleep, sir."

The Writer's head throbbed when he replied, "That's very polite for you to put it that way, Mr. Portafoy. But the truth is I cavorted with those rambunctious girls all night, drank to excess, and now I'm hungover. Thank you for the offer, but I think I can handle it..."

"Very good, sir. Have a good day, sir." And then Portafoy left the cramped laundry room.

The Writer had been tempted to accept the offer—and to pay, of course—but who knew what kind of "skidmarks" existed in his shorts? Not to mention the suspicious and ill-smelling dampness of his jeans. *That's right. I pissed my pants last night. Bravo.*

And much else transpired last night as well, correct?

Fuck, thought the Writer amid the "slug-slug-slug" of the Maytag. He tried to focus his wincing memory...

Did the old man—Septimus—die last night? He pinched his bearded chin. *Or was that a dream?* The doppelganger had said so too, hadn't he? And the Writer still didn't know what to make of *him.*

He stared his thoughts down. *Wait a minute. The Bighead. THAT'S no dream—I saw the corpse. And now...the corpse is gone... Dawn claims that "someone" unlocked the funeral parlor doors, rejuvenated the thing's blood supply, and let it out.* More staring. *That thing—the Bighead—walked out of that embalming suite after being dead on the slab for twenty years.*

What did the Writer propose to do about that?

He rejected the idea of further deliberation on the conundrums encircling him: Was he insane? Was all this a dream? Was there really a monster thrashing through the woods right now, and was there really a doppelganger? *Fuck it. I'm not worrying about it.* The washing machine slug-slug-slugged on. *I don't care. I will take the day as it comes.*

Once the wash cycle finished, he crammed it all in the dryer, returned briefly to his room, put several things in a plastic Safeway bag, and left. Descending the stairs, he smiled at one of the "Howard" sketches, knowing now who it really was, and thrilled in the knowledge that, however vaguely, he was walking where H.P. Lovecraft had once walked. The supposition recurred. *I'm a millionaire now—I could afford child support easily. If I knocked Snowie up, my kid would share the same bloodline as Howard Phillips Lovecraft!*

A silly thought, but an interesting one. And, "of a sudden," as M.R. James might say, simply the errant idea of jettisoning a great big ejaculation into Snowie's probably-well-used-loins for the sole purpose of siring a child with his genes and some of Lovecraft's, well, *that* notion spurred a more physical reaction: a spontaneous erection. *Wow, instant hard-on. Not bad for sixty!*

By the time he arrived in the lobby, a fair shake of pre-ejaculatory fluid was introducing itself into his shorts, and then, when he turned the corner—BAM—more such fluid eddied out at the sight of Mrs. Howard behind the front desk. *Great Odin's ghost! Would you get a load of the TITS on that woman!*

The statuesque albino smiled over at his entrance. She wore one of her omnipresent sun dresses which had a way of making a *perfect* presentation of her bosom. No brassiere was in evidence, nor did there seem to be a need for one. The orbicular double-D's stood out high and mighty with no trace of sag. *Tits that mean business,* came the Writer's immediate and quite crude reflection. *Fuck.* His now-uncomfortably arranged erection bumped up another notch in turgidity, and out leaked more "drool."

When she turned, her elongated face lit up, and the angle by which she'd turned brought her visage in near-perfect alignment with another, larger framed sketch or engraving of Lovecraft on the wall behind her. The similarity of the facial structures was uncanny. *Lovecraft's sperm was packing some STRONG genes.* Not that Lovecraft's exceedingly long face and protuberant jaw made for a pleasing combination when atop a curvaceous and very well-endowed woman. *Not exactly feminine, nor "pretty,"* he concluded but still...a fascinating dichotomy. A further ridiculous muse: *If I had sex with her or Snowie...I'd be looking down at H.P. Lovecraft's face! It would almost be like I was banging him!*

"And good afternoon to you, Mr. Writer!" The woman beamed. "How are you this fine day?"

I'm hungover as hell and I've got an aching erection that your magnificent cleavage is only making ache more... "I couldn't be better, Mrs. Howard."

"Good. Let me offer you a treat." She reached lower, and set on the counter a bowl of candy.

"Why, thank you," he said and reached for the bowl...but then stopped via an abrupt inner-monitor...

She was offering a bowl of Gummy Worms.

The Writer clenched at the recollection.

Mrs. Howard whooped laughter. "Gotcha with that, didn't I? Couldn't resist!"

"You got me all right," he said dully. The hangover had pushed aside many of last night's charming details, like the scam Mrs. Howard and Snowie were running. They'd hidden cameras in some of the larger rooms, hoping to record activities for which patrons might later be inclined to pay "ransom." Last night's footage had to be the cream of the crop: the evangelical Pastor Tommy Ignatius watching kiddie porn and masturbating whilst inserting Gummy Worms into his penis. *What a wonderfully diverse world we live in!*

"I'll pass on the Gummy Worms, ma'am. But speaking of the like, where is our good friend Pastor Tommy?"

"Oh, he was up early as a bird and out the door, said he was goin' fer a walk to thank the Lord for this fine day and all the blessins of this life."

The Writer smiled. *He went for a walk straight to June's Spa to get a rubber dick stuffed up his ass by a girl who's probably sixteen...* A vengeful person the Writer was not, nor a judgmental one, but there came a certain point when simple common sense must be engaged. *The guy's a phony pastor, and he beats off looking at kiddie porn, and I'd say the probability is rather high that if such a man LOOKS at naked children, he's probably MOLESTED at least a few himself. If there is a God, as I think I believe there is, I'd say the good pastor is putting himself in the way of a good pranging from the Man upstairs.* "Vengeance is mine, I will repay," saith the Lord." The immortal quote, particularly in this instance, had a snappy ring to it.

But, lo, where might that leave the Writer?

This brief inner reflection rang grimly. *I cream-pied a corpse the other night. I drink more than Hemingway and Sherwood Anderson combined, and I lust with a fury over Snowie and Dawn.* The Writer gulped. *Where does that leave me, in God's eyes?*

He ground away the supposal. *I guess I better get my spiritual shit together...*

"It just makes me wonder," said Mrs. Howard slowly, cheek in palm.

"What's that, Mrs. Howard?"

"What makes fellas wanna stick things in their peckers?"

"I assure you, I haven't a clue, and I look forward never to acquainting myself with the sensation unless I live long enough to go into a nursing home and get catheterized."

But Mrs. Howard seemed in a fog. "And where the *hail* did all them Gummy Worms go? He must'a slid four or five of 'em in there. They go up into his bladder, ya think? Did he pee 'em out later?"

"I regret to say that your erudite questions can only be answered by a quicker intelligence than mine, Mrs. Howard. But if I may change the subject, did Snowie go to work today?"

The large-breasted woman chuckled. "That dumb-bunny daughter'a mine? More tits than brains, I say. Yeah, you should'a seen her limpin' out of here..."

Yes, the Writer recalled—not that he could forget. *The cunt-kicking contest last night in Backtown...*

He'd HAVE to put that in the book.

He bid Mrs. Howard a good day (just as his eyes bid her *cleavage* a good day), and the next five minutes found him strolling down Main Street in warm sunlight. Passersby—perfect strangers—all waved cheerily at him. *That's right. I'm The One, the town saviur of backwoods legendry and local lore, the figure of good omen, the Blessing Incarnate.* But such stories were nothing new, and people had been inventing them since cave-man days. *If I really am the town's savior, then time will tell. And I will be facing something far worse than the 91st Psalm's "Pestilence that walketh in Dark."*

It sounded like bullshit to him but, again, time would tell.

He enjoyed his afternoon's perambulation. His headache dissipated quickly, and imparted a sudden elevation in his mood, while an unbidden thought of Snowie imparted a sudden elevation of his reproductive apparatus. *Damn, this dick! It's not supposed to be doing this at my age!*

Ambling on toward the gas station, he found himself peering at the mild ascent of Main Street with more scrutiny than would be deemed normal.

Of course—Septimus Howard's story of the Cubbler twins, a pair of fourteen-year-olds "but with racks'a boobs on 'em like they was both full-grown adults, and I kin tell ya sure as I is old, them two had tits that could stop a train," the old man had assured. He'd also said that a number of years ago, these twins had spent Halloween night on Crafter's property, with Ouija boards, black candles, and other occult accouterments, whereupon they'd attempted to compel communication with the dead and had evidently gotten more than they'd bargained for.

It was on this self-same road, and just about this same exactly place that, the following morning, both of these girls trudged trancelike, and utterly naked.

They were both, too, utterly pregnant, sporting full-term bellies, whereas not twelve hours earlier, they'd both been utterly UNpregnant. Indeed, most witnesses concurred that if anything, the young blondes were *more* than full-term; they were what one would be if subject to the impossible condition of being ten or even *twelve* months pregnant, so great and distended were their bellies.

Moments later, they'd stopped, with mouths agape and eyes wide as saucers, while an appalled crowd gathered. Then they'd both parted their legs, looked to the clear blue sky, and began to *heave*, ejecting from their throats sounds of anguish only partly human.

The Writer stared forward as the details of the story refreshed themselves in his mind, and for a moment he could very much *see* the diabolic spectacle with his own eyes: the blondes convulsing, red-faced, blue veins throbbing at their necks, as the great gravid bellies quickly collapsed, transferring the wares of those bellies onto the surface of Main Street: not two babies but two *piles* of indescribable matter, and each pile *had* to weigh fifty pounds.

The stench from the two mounds was worse than anything any of the spectators had ever smelled. Some even passed out as the street cleared. Ten or fifteen years ago this had occurred; no one knew for sure because no one wanted to remember. One universal comment was made of the stench of the two piles: "It was not a stench from this earth." One old timer remarked, "'Twas the *devil's shit...,* it shore as hail was! As if Satan himself took a giant shit up both them girls' pussies and filled 'em up like a pair'a sandbags when a flood's a-comin'!"

The Cubbler twins lived on to this day, in a county mental hospital, staring out their windows, mouths hung open, silent for all these years.

The Writer blinked, and felt winded when this mental mirage came to a terminus. *Wow. That's some tale. Jack London's got NOTHING on that.* But did the Writer believe it?

I...think I do, he thought. *Bombastic, over-the-top, reeking of incredulity—yes. But then, so is the tale of the Bighead, and I saw the thing's corpse yesterday, just as sure as I'm seeing the asphalt on this street now...*

But there were things to do now, so he got his mind off the arabesque and reset it on the concrete world. His To-Do List remained ever-present in his cognizance:

1) Pick up my hot rod at garage.
2) Buy shovel at hardware store.
3) Bring Voynich page.
4) Pick up Snowie and Dawn.
5) Drive to Crafter House on Governor's Bridge Road.
6) Find grave and dig up Crafter's body.

Well, he had the Voynich page in his Safeway bag, along with his laptop and some other items that might come in handy.

A few minutes' walk brought him to the foot of the gas station where men had worked all night to refurbish Dicky Caudill's old black El Camino. But now it was the Writer's old *white* El Camino, looking brand new sitting just outside of the first bay. The Writer never cared about cars, much less hot rods, but he had to admit, *this* car looked sharp, and it made him feel a bit younger now that he owned it. But here was the hardware store just across the street. *Might as well get the shovel first.*

A cowbell rang when he entered the front door of Worden's Hardware Store, and an instantaneous coincidence occurred to him. The clue that had led police to the home of Wisconsin serial-killer Ed Gein had been a carbon-paper receipt for one gallon of anti-freeze at a "Worden's Hardware Store," in Plainfield, owned by a Mrs. Bernice Worden, who had been reported missing previously. Mr. Gein had, also previously, signed the receipt. Not too much in the way of smarts. Mrs. Worden, by the way, was found stripped, headless, hung upside-down, cleaved open from vagina to sternum later that day.

Ah, but this was not Plainfield, Wisconsin; it was Luntville, West Virginia, and the aforementioned coincidence has virtually no bearing on this story...

So, the Writer entered the hardware store behind the cheery bell, took a few steps forward, and stopped as if at a sudden alarm.

I've seen this place before...

Yes, he had.

He'd seen this self-same store last night in one of his dreams. *It looks identical,* he thought, *but that's probably just the power of suggestion. Let's see if there's a paint-shaker here;* because the keynote event of last night's dream had been the Larkins boys clamping a man's head into an old fashioned power paint-shaker in order to effect brain damage.

The idea was to turn the man into a "Ricky Retardo," but evidently they set the machine too high and the meth-dealing victim had died. Not so, however, the machine's first victim, a curvaceous but reed-thin blonde. They'd stripped her naked, clamped her head into the machine for a half-minute, and, *presto!* Instant retardate fuck-dummy! And fuck her they had, with vigor, and they did not confine the ventures of their erections to the gibbering woman's vagina alone...

The Writer walked to the front of the musty store, hoping there'd be no paint-shaker.

There was a paint-shaker at one end of the front counter.

The Writer frowned.

"Can I help ya, fella?" a husky voice asked. The Writer turned to face a tall 300-pound man with a blond buzzcut. *Finally,* the Writer thought, *I've come face to face with one of the infamous Larkins brothers.*

"Yes, actually. I'm in dire need of nothing more or less than a plain old every-day type shovel."

Monsieur Larkins (this one went by the name of Gut, by the way; his three identical brothers were Clyde, Tucker, and Horace), started, "Ever-kind of shovel you could ever want, right over there in aisle—" Then he gasped, did a double take, slapped both meaty palms down on the counter top, and exclaimed, "Why, good golly holy mosey, sir! I know you!"

"You're likely incorrect. I'm sure we've never met."

"Naw, naw, I mean I could tell by your aura—"

The Writer gawped. *My AURA! What kind of observation is THAT for a King-Kong-sized sociopathic redneck to make?*

Gut Larkins *slapped* a giant palm down on the counter. "That's it! You're the One, ain't ya? Fella that started Dicky Caudill's car 'n ended the curse?"

The Writer wilted a bit. "Like the King Arthur legend, yes, that's what quite a number of people have in mind, but I don't know…"

"Here ya go, sir," another voice surprised him, and there, standing hugely, was another quadruplet, holding a 47-inch ash-handled Tru Temper shovel. "Best shovel in the house."

"Why, that should suffice perfectly, thanks." The Writer leaned the shovel against the counter and consulted his wallet.

"That there's a tin roof, sir," interjected Gut.

The other one chuckled. "Yeah, ya know? On the house?"

The Writer thought he'd heard that one before. "Well, really, I appreciate your generosity but I feel I should pay—"

"No, sir. After all you done fer us? We cain't take nothin' from the One. Your money's no good here."

"Well, okay, thank you very much…"

"No, thank *you,* sir, and you go have yourself a happy diggin'."

The Writer made to leave but halted upon noticing something at the end of the counter. "Why, that machine there?" he inquired.

"Isn't that an old—"

Now the other two quadruplets appeared, huge and all smiles. One said, "That there's a paint-shaker, sir. Leftover from the old days. They got all these new-fangled ways'a mixin' paint nowadays. But ya ask me? Old ways is best ways."

"Yes, I, uh, happen to agree," said the Writer. "In these corporate times, it's all Home Depot and Lowe's, I imagine. But I don't suppose you have much occasion to use that, do you?"

The fourth brother patted the machine with a hand the size of Andre the Giant's (if you even *remember* Andre the Giant). "'S'matter of fact, sir, we done used it just a short spell ago, didn't we fellas?"

The three others chuckled, grinning. "Shore did," one acknowledged—maybe Tucker, maybe Clyde, but it really didn't fuckin' matter. "We shook us UP some paint, oh yeah!"

And of this, Writer suspected he was all too aware. *Sixty years old and now I'm having clairvoyant dreams.* But why not have some fun with this? He stiffened, closed his eyes, and put a hand to his temple. "I see, I see…a man. Portly but with skinny legs, in shorts. He looks a little bit like a cross between that comedian Pauly Shore, and Richard Simmons. I sense…he's an ex-convict and drug dealer. And then—yes!—I see…a *woman!* A blonde! And-and, she's *naked,* very slightly built, and she's staggering, yes, like a zombie…"

The Writer pretended to snap out of it. He sighed as if dizzied, his eyes fluttered. "Wow, sorry. Happens every now and then—I have the strangest visions that make absolutely no sense."

The four brothers all stood wide-eyed and staring with mouths opened.

"Probably one of my blood-pressure meds," said the Writer. "The doctor said things like that might happen. An annoying side-effect. Well, gentlemen, I'm off, and thank you for the shovel. I bid you all a splendid day."

The cowbell rang when he left the store. *That was fun,* he thought. But he considered the circumstance no further. There was work to do.

As he approached DeHenzel's garage, someone else approached as well, from the opposite direction.

"Dawn!" exclaimed the Writer, genuinely happy to see her. The well-endowed mortician, however, looked anything but happy—she looked as one overwhelmed by dread. The Writer tried to appear sympathetic to her expression but this was impossible as she was wearing tight jeans and one of her OD-green Army t-shirts which strained before monumental braless breasts. *I could have a heart-attack just LOOKING at those...* "I was just about to call you but... judging by your expression, you seem distressed. What's wrong?"

"What's wrong?!" she yelped. "Don't you remember last night?"

"Why, yes, I do. I remember drinking to excess. I remember chatting with Septimus Howard. And I remember you and Snowie in a cunt-kicking contest."

"The Bighead, you dummy! He's on the loose!"

"Oh, ah, yes—that!" stammered the Writer. "Of course, I recall your information last night. Someone broke into the mortuary, then broke into the special vault, and—"

"Yeah! Then they pumped out all of the Bighead's embalming fluid and replaced it with his original blood supply, and then he came back to life and walked out of the place!"

"Yes," the Writer assented, nodding.

She grimaced. "You act like you don't believe me!"

The Writer tried hard to look her in the face, but the task was unachievable; all her could visually focus on were those two outrageous breasts straining within the t-shirt. "If you want to know the truth, Dawn, the scariest thing of all is that I DO believe you." And then, in thought, *And I even know who did it, but there's one story NO ONE will believe.* "But before we can do anything about it, we need answers first. Now, we're going to—"

Dawn seemed bewildered and offended. "You're talking to *me* but looking at my *tits*."

"I know! I'm sorry, I can't help it. I don't know what's come over me lately but—"

Her eyes sparked over a lewd grin. "I sure as fuck wish *I* could come over you."

His erection made an aggravating throb at the words. "Can't you just, I don't know—put a different shirt on?"

"No. Snowie thinks *she's* going to get you, but fuck her. You're *mine*."

"For shit's sake! I'm a burned out fat old man. Now stop distracting me! First, we have to pick up my car, then we gotta pick up Snowie."

"Fuck her! She can't go anywhere anyway, she's working."

This the Writer disregarded. "I think my newly filled wallet can persuade her to quit that job at the convenience store, and the same goes for you too. Both you girls are working for me now. A hundred a day, cash, plus, when we're finished with the tasks ahead, I'll buy each of you a brand-new car, just like I promised last night."

At once the Writer was being smothered by her affections; his head was yanked to hers, her tongue invading his mouth and roving maniacally, her breasts pressed to his chest such that he could feel her heart beating, and her hand already down his pants coddling his genitals and squeezing out a great rivulet of pre-ejaculatory ooze.

"Stop stop stop stop stop!" he snapped, twisting out of her grasp. "You're gonna make me come in my pants!"

"So?" she said.

"We can't do this standing in the middle of Main Street in broad daylight! Now come on!" and he grabbed her hand and towed her toward the garage.

"Your keys, sir," said the tall shaggy blond man in a mechanic's jumpsuit. "'Twas an honor to work on it, sir. She's runs like a dream. You won't believe it. Had this place full'a mechanics all night long. Bet it runs better'n the day it rolled outta the showroom."

"Thank very much." He took the keys, tossed them to Dawn, and said, "you drive." Then, back to DeHenzel, "Do I owe you any more money?"

"No, sir, and to be honest I owe you a refund of about fifteen grand. Thought after all them years the engine'd have to be replaced but, nothin' doin'. Whole block, rockers, rings—everything was clean as a whistle."

"You don't say..."

"Dickey Caudill knew how to take care of an engine, he did. Of course, all the wires, plugs, belts, points, and all else is brand new, the best stuff." The blond man pulled out a checkbook. "Lemme get'cha your refund—"

The Writer eyed him intently. "Keep it. Thanks for your time, honesty, and expertise."

"Yes, sir! A pleasure, sir. Anything ever go wrong with that car, you bring it right back to me." Then he paused, as if in recollection. "Oh, forgot somethin', sir. When we was on break yesterday, we saw your son rummagin' around in the car, but he didn't do no mischief, and we figured it was okay with you."

"You have a son!" Dawn wailed.

"No! Be quiet! I'll tell you later," he snapped at her. "Yes, yes," he replied to DeHenzel. "That's fine. Have a good day."

That fuckin' doppelganger, what a pain in the ass! But his irritation ceased in an instant when he took his first close look at the refurbished car. Once obsidian-black but now as white as a glacier, shimmering beneath ten coats of lacquer. Inside looked brand-new as well, down to every detail, every panel, pieces of rubber trim. The long bench seat had been expertly re-upholstered with leather. Everything was spotless.

"This...is impressive," the Writer remarked, now installed on the passenger side.

"You have a son!" Dawn wailed again. "Damn you!"

"I don't have a son," he growled. "It's just some guy who looks like me, and it's too long a story to go into."

"And I'll bet you're married too! Fuck you!"

"Dawn, I swear to every deity known to humankind, I am *not* married, nor will I ever be."

"Yeah? Well, we'll see about that—hey, look over here! You're not even looking!"

What now? He looked over at her behind the wheel and was struck by an image as abrupt as a poke in the eye.

Dawn had peeled her green U.S. Army t-shirt up over her breasts.

The Writer's erection throbbed again. "Put those away!" he yelled and reached to pull her shirt back down, but in doing so, his hand—either accidentally or unconsciously—squeezed one massive, gravity-defying breast.

"You just copped a feel!" she giggled.

"That's...not altogether true." He put his hand back in his lap and—either accidentally or subconsciously, or maybe on purpose—squeezed his own crotch, and felt another well of pre-ejaculatory fluid empty into his shorts.

"What's all that shit in the Safeway bag?" she asked.

"My laptop and some other things we might need on hand." He couldn't resist. From the bag he withdraw the rotten Hand of Glory and showed it to her. "Get it? On *hand?*"

"What the fuck is that!?"

"The severed left hand of an executed murderer, an infamous occult totem. They call it the Hand of Glory, and it's said to open any lock. It was with this arcane implement, I believe, that our perpetrator entered your mortuary last night, re-animated the Bighead, and provided for the thing's escape."

Dawn eyed him. "The tone of your voice sounds like you know who the 'perpetrator' is..."

"I think I do," he admitted. "But you wouldn't understand. It stems from mysticism and a bunch of literary shit. You wouldn't understand. Let's get going, we gotta pick up Snowie, and then get down to business." The Writer handed her the keys.

"But I thought only the One could drive the car," she posed.

This he considered. "I have the notion that since I ended the curse, anyone can now drive the car with my permission. The mechanics were able to test drive it, so...start 'er up."

Dawn depressed the clutch, turned the key, then the engine ROARED to life. The sound was so tumultuous, the Writer nearly shouted out loud.

"Now *that's* an engine!" Dawn celebrated.

Her awesome breasts jerked when she shifted into first, then—

Inertia slammed the Writer back into his seat, and this time he *did indeed* shout out loud as the tires screeched interminably, the back-end fish-tailed, and the smoke of burning rubber drew two lines down Main Street.

***

—a distant screeching sound...

Something seemed to be growing in his skull, and then the thought surfaced: *Tires. On the road. Them round things on what they call cars. Spinnin' fast...* Then the screeching noises drifted away.

The Bighead didn't know shit just yet but it seemed that with every step his—or its—huge yellow-brown feet took though the woods, a smidgen more knowledge presented itself to his—or its—consciousness. For instance, (we'll just go with *he* from here on), last night when he'd got hisself off'a that big table and walked outta that place with all them grey walls, he didn't remember nothin' about hisself, but now he was a-startin' to remember stuff, and cool stuff most of it was. Like bustin' the nut in some splittail's cooze, and the way them gals'd scream while he was poundin' it out. See, the Bighead's cock were so long'n fat (big around as a strong man's forearm, and as long), it'd tear their pussies up and bust things deep inside 'em. A'course, the Bighead didn't have nothin' against the gals personal...

But, hail, a nut were a nut. 'Sides, way back a long time ago, when Grandpap were raisin' him up down in the Lower Woods, Grandpap tole Bighead right off that it was all's right to kill people and ruck 'em up with his big pecker 'cos they'se was all folks from the Outside World, and what that meant was it meant they was all evil, so's it were a right thing ta fuck 'em and eat 'em. And that were fine with the Bighead, yes sir. He didn't think on the whys'n wherefores—he just knowed that when his belly were empty, it was just dandy to fill it up again with the meat he pulled off'a folks, and it were a dandy thing too ta bloody up a splittail's pussy and fill it up. Felt so *good*, it did, when all that peckersnot were'a pumpin' fierce outta that big dick'a his.

The Bighead tromped onward through the woods, naked, monstrous, and, well, happy as hell.

He et well off'a that splittail he'd come across last night, after, a'course, fuckin' her ta high heaven. Her baby-hole made a neat crunching sound when he was poundin' into it, and you can bet she were a bloody mess when he was done. Big river'a blood flowed outta her pussy along with a slightly smaller river'a cum. Bighead pried open her ribs bare-handed and et the meat off 'em, then he wolfed down the liver. He yanked the intestines out of her gut like a bunch'a hot, squishy rope—his favorite part—and sucked the shit out of 'em whiles it were still hot. Bighead gnawed on the butt-meat awhile, then his breadbasket was full up, and he felt a right dandy. Bighead never would'a guessed it was his first meal in over twenty years.

And onward he went, through the nighted forest, not knowing where he was going but going just the same. A little after he put that ruckin' on the gal, the Bighead crossed paths with a hobblin' old man. His football-sized heart surged in a sudden joy because, see, at first the Bighead thought the old man was his Grandpap, but as his slowly regenerating brain worked up some synaptic activity, the Bighead then remembered that his Grandpap had died a long time ago when they both lived down in the Lower Woods. But could this man be, perhaps, Grandpap's ghost, come to Earth to bid good tidings to the Bighead?

Aw, fuck no! Grandpap only had one arm and this here oldster had two, plus Grandpap had hisself a billy-goat type goatee, while this other fella had a beard two feet long like those guys in ZZ Top (not that Bighead knew who ZZ Top was), so, pretty much just for the hell of it, the Bighead yanked that beard right off the old man's face, but the old man probably didn't feel nothin' 'cos it looked to Bighead like the codger died right off. He just let out a wavering scream, and died just as that beard tore right out of his face. Bighead didn't have a fancy ta eat any of him on account he'd just et not too long ago, but he pulled the geezer apart limb from proverbial limb anyway, and pulled his old dick off too.

Why?

Well, it seemed like the right thing to do.

But that had all been last night, and by now, trudgin' through the bright sunlight, the Bighead was workin' up a mighty thirst. Past the next hollow, shimmering creek water shone, glinting in dappled sunlight. Bighead stepped right up and knelt right down, lowering his big dog-toothed maw into the cool, unspoiled water, and he gulped down a couple of gallons, he did. On the last swallow, however, he hacked something up that had gone into his mouth. He spat it into his huge hand, and peered inquisitively, somehow fascinated.

What the object was, exactly, was a prophylactic, and one into which some male contributor had already expended a respectable portion of sperm—(proof that the water wasn't exactly *unspoiled*). A'course, the Bighead didn't know what the *hail* a fuckin' prophylactic was, but he sure knew nut when he saw it, and here was plenty, all a-hangin' at the end of this little rubber sleeve-like thing. Well, Bighead upended that fucker and sucked that rotten sperm right onto his great flap of a tongue.

Now, jest because he'd et cum plenty of times in the past, don't git ta deducin' that the Bighead were some kind'a homah-sexshul. No, sir! He *always* preferred fuckin' a gal more'n a fella, and, hail, a nut's a nut, ain't it? S'all "pank on the inside," as folks is fond'a sayin. And in the old days, shee-it, he'd sucked *plenty* of peckersnot out of dead gals' pussies and butts, not just dead fellas' butts. So what's the big to-do? He liked the taste'a cum in a big way! Some folks like the taste'a okra, and some don't. Some like the taste'a corn cakes, and others fuckin' don't. Well, same thing here. Some liked the taste'a nut, some didn't. Big deal! 'Twas all a matter'a taste! Folks just didn't get it!

Yes, and all day long now, he'd been rememberin' more'n more about hisself, when last night he could barely remember a blammed thing! And last night, it didn't seem like he could see jack shit out of his little eye, just the big one, yet now he thought he was startin' to see things out the little one too, and, what the fuck? Last night, the little one hadn't been nothin' more'n a hole in his head! Somethin' a damn sight *untoward* seemed to be takin' place, what with so many memories comin' back, and his eyesight. In fact, last night, he'd stuck his almost-foot-long finger inta the big hole in the back of his head, and there weren't much inside his skull...

But *now?*

Half that empty space were now filt *up* with soft squishy stuff, which the Bighead reckoned was his *brain.* Yes, sir! It *had* to be that his brain were growin' back inside his skull!

If poor old Grandpap was still kickin', why, he'd say fer shore that this were a miracle'a God!

But...Bighead seriously doubted that God had anything ta do with it.

Moments of reflection seemed like a jarring incongruity for a being like the Bighead, yet reflect he did, hunched down there with his giant feet in the pristine water, painted by shifting sunlight through the leaves overhead, nestled in the very cusp of nature's beauty. But now it was time to consider a less subjective kind of reflection (not that Bighead knew what the *fuck* subjective meant) and that would be the *physical* reflection of his face in the surface of the creek.

Tar-NAY-tions!

The Bighead got a jolt, he did, when he got a look at his face. If it were possible for Bighead to think thoughts in human words, he would've thought something like this: *I is one UGLY motherfucker!*

Ugly was the word, all right: *bigtime* ugly. Shit, no wonder the old man had died last night just from lookin' at him! Bighead's head sat on his shoulders like a lopsided watermelon—like, a *thirty-pound* watermelon—and hadda mouth on it more like a lightning crater... that is a crater with fangs as of a very large dog. Tiny little squiggles of flesh comprised his ears, and then of course came his eyes, the big one and the little one that was just a hole in his head now. Yes, he'd been shot a long time ago, hadn't he?—shot with a pistol by a man in black clothes and a white collar, and the bullet (a Federal 455, for those interested) had hit him right smack-dab in that eye and blowed most'a his brains out the back of his head. Perhaps glimpsing his horrific reflection had dislodged the long buried memory, or perhaps...

Aw, what the fuck difference did it make?

The big eye was big around as a tennis ball, but had no visible iris or pupil. It just looked grayish and slimy, like a plop of raw oysters. Now, however, he noticed that somethin' grayish was indeed growing in the hole that had once been the abode for his little eye. Just as he thunk: that eye was *a-growin' back* just like his brain. Hence, he wasn't quite as distraught as he had been after seein' how sure-fire *ugly* he was, and, yeah, it'd be a lot nicer if he looked more like folks hereabouts, but, hail, come ta think of it, Bighead had a lot to be grateful for!

So no more moping about his looks!

Bighead stomped outta that creek water and thundered on, standin' tall and proud'a himself even with him bein' far, far uglier than, say, an orangutan's ass. Yes, sir! Standin' tall! Beauty, they say, was on the inside!

The Bighead moseyed on in his long, monstrous strides. Rabbits, squirrels, skunks, and other such wildlife all popped up their heads, looked at Bighead, then ran away faster than they'd ever run in their small mammalian lives. And—no lie—an owl hooted at him from a high tree, and when Bighead looked up at it, that poor birds squawked once, croaked on the spot, and fell with a plop onto the ground below. Damn! *That's* how ugly the Bighead was.

But his feelings wasn't hurt even a tad. N'fact, once a long time ago, Grandpap told Bighead about some fella named Moses goin' up ta some mountain ta meet God, but, see, God hadda appear to Moses as a burning bush on account, well, the *true* face'a God were "inscrutable," (that's what Grandpap said: *inscrutable*) "And ya see, Bighead," Grandpap explained, "that means the face'a God on High is *so complex* and *so beyond our understandin'* that a human cain't even *look* at God's face without up'n *dyin'!* So that thar's why He turnt Hisself inta a burnin' bush!"

Bighead considered this on a positive note. The eye-deer, see, leant some weight to the notion that he and God had somethin' in common!

Bighead plodded on but stopped abruptly at a smell. It was plainly the smell of excrement, freshly produced. This odor, by the way, offensive to humans, did not offend the Bighead in any way, shape, or form. To the contrary, he *liked* this odor; in fact, it was to him as delectable as the aromas of, say, Thanksgiving dinner would be to a person. But...

Where is this observation going?

Ah, yes. In another long step, the source of the shit-smell appeared, here, by a corroded tree stump: nothing more than a pile of fecal matter, and a sizable pile at that. No doubt some beast of nature had done its business and moved on. Only…

It was a *big* pile, seriously. Not even the Bighead took shits *that* big.

Next observation: a chorus of tiny squeals. Immediately, the Bighead thought of a nest of baby birds even though the sound didn't quite agree with that comparison. Bighead noticed a hole in the side of a long-dried-out creekbed.

Being that this was the Bighead's first "jaunt" in over twenty years, he found himself possessed by a rather inquiring turn; in fact, he felt it necessary to discover the source of the tiny squealing and to also discern the nature and purpose in the hole alongside the old creekbed.

He lumbered his pallid-yellow and gray-and brown-splotched naked body down into the ravine. He stuck his huge head into the hole.

Of all things!

There, recessed in the hole, nestled quite cutely, was a litter of four tiny baby black bears—"cubs," they would be called, and the hole, of course, was a "den." Since Bighead was a hybrid (part human and part something else) his one fully functioning eye could see in even pitch darkness, and, oh, what an adorable sight were these baby bears: cute little bundles of fur. Fortunately, it was so dark that the pups themselves couldn't see Bighead; otherwise, they probably would've croaked just like the owl…so horrifically butt-ugly was the Bighead's visage.

And his first instinct here was strangely unexpected. The Bighead's wont had always been to kill *every living thing* that crossed his path, and he still felt bound to that. Like Grandpap had said: "Ain't nothin' good nowhere on this airth, so's ya might as well tear the livin' shit out of ever-thang ya see." And he was going to do just that when such opportunities presented themselves. As for this den of little baby bears—why, Bighead could swallow 'em whole if he wanted to, or just squish 'em up for the hell of it if'n he wasn't hungry.

But...

No, wouldn't be right to do that. The little critters were just too cute. He took one last adoring look at them, then pulled his head out of the hole.

Now, Bighead was no zoologist, and it didn't really occur to him that wherever there might be little baby bears there was sure to be also a big honking *mama bear* in very close proximity, and this natural fact made itself evident the moment Bighead stepped up out of that ravine.

The Bighead was not capable of experiencing that emotion known as fear...but he had to admit he felt a bit of a shock when he stood back upright and found himself facing the bellowing, wide-open maw of a 900-pound American Black Bear. The animal's objection to the Bighead was more than plain, and the roar which was ejected from its gargantuan throat seemed as loud as a jet turbine. Bighead could not recall a time in his foggy past that he'd encountered any living thing bigger than himself—but this bear was it, and at once, the twenty-pound pile of excrement noted previously was explained. The Bighead didn't want to be part of the next pile, and of course, his hybrid killing machine instincts engaged immediately, and he hurled one volley-ball-sized fist in a great arc, smacking the bear in the side of the head.

The bear wobbled, mewled, and flopped over with an audible *THUD!*

So much for the bear's ferocious defense of its den. But the blow hadn't killed the beast; it was still breathing and clearly knocked unconscious.

The next instinct, of course, was to tear the bear's heart out and eat it. However...

Those tiny squeals from the litter of baby bears could still easily be heard, and the Bighead reckoned that if he killed the mother bear, those defenseless babies would be carried off in minutes by predators.

Well, the Bighead couldn't have that; those little critters were simply too cute. So he resolved to go on about his business...

...but only *after* he had sodomized the mother bear, apparently for good measure. It was the Bighead's view that what the bear didn't know wouldn't hurt her.

***

The white El Camino's stout engine noise through the chambered exhaust and Hooker headers established command of the road—Tick Neck Road, to be precise. Over winding asphalt roads and swooshing through dense, rising woods and a primeval forests that brought to mind Lovecraft's "Dunwich Horror" and "The Lurking Fear."

Aside, there was something *lurking*, too, in the Writer's pants because at that very moment he was sitting on the passenger side. While Snowie, whom they'd recently picked up at her convenience store, was sitting in his lap, using the excuse that if she sat between him and Dawn, then Dawn wouldn't be able to effectively shift gears. This assertion, however, was too severe a view; in truth, there was more than enough room between him and Dawn, but this Snowie refused to hear, and since the author of this narrative has already expended far too many words than are called for on this situation, we'll move on…

So engrossed was Dawn in the operation of this penultimate hot rod that she noticed nothing of the activities to her right. Snowie, deliberately, of course, was grinding her plush blue-jeaned rump over the Writer's groin, and she alternately tried to stuff her hand down his pants. He must've snatched it away a dozen times, each time snapping "Stop it! Stop it!" at which she simply laughed and continued her mischief. Snowie's crinkly white hair smelled lovely, like herbal shampoo, and this, along with the grinding movements of her buttocks, only furthered his sexual arousal.

Shit, my dick feels like six inches of lead pipe! and if this were the case, then that pipe needed a plumber because it was leaking copiously.

Next, she grabbed both of his hands and plopped them on her breasts. "Feel these up," she giggled, and she giggled more when he tried to pull his hands away and came to the pathetic conclusion that she was stronger than him. *What a fat, weak old putz I am,* he resigned. Unable to move his hands he just shrugged and began rubbing her breasts, then kneading them, then tweezing her nipples through the fabric of her blouse. Snowie purred approvingly, grinding her buttocks harder against his groin. He yowled when she quickly stuffed her hand between her legs and then between his, to rub manically. "Stop it! Stop it!" he barked. "You're gonna make me ejaculate in my pants!"

"Then pull your cock out and you can ejaculate in my mouth," she said.

"Just...STOP molesting me!"

Dawn turned her grin to the current antics, finally cognizant of what was going on. "Just wait 'til we get to where we're going. I'll give you a *real* set of tits to squeeze."

"Yeah?" Snowie said. "And I'll give you a real *foot* up your ass, instead of that fake one you got."

"Second thing I do when we get to where we're going," Dawn replied, "is haul your pussy inside out and take a shit on your fuckin' uterus. Then I'll whup you upside the head with my *fake foot* and knock the retard out of you."

The Writer saw another fight coming; he didn't want his new hot rod wrecked on its first trip—so he yelled, actually with some authority: "Shut up, both of you! Right now, you're both working for *me!* If you want to get paid, and if you both want a brand new car, there will be NO MORE FIGHTING! You understand?"

Both girls nodded reluctantly.

"Any more of this bickering nonsense," he added, "and who knows? I just might kick both your asses myself."

Dawn and Snowie looked at each other, paused, and erupted into a long burst of hysterical laughter.

The Writer frowned. *They know I'm a weakling and an old pud. Who am I kidding?* "All right, you've both had your laugh of the day. Now let's get back to my mission unless you want me to give those brand new cars to two *other* girls."

This prompted the desired effect: silence. *Silentium est aureum,* the Writer thought with a smile.

(As a side note, it may be worth mentioning—or perhaps not—that in his rare tirade, he'd forgotten to remove his hands from Snowie's magnificent breasts, which he still continued to knead like hot dough.)

Snowie said with enthusiasm, "Oh, Dawn, I forgot to tell you. Last night we had the cam on in Pastor Tommy's room and he was beatin' off sticking gummy worms in his dick!"

Dawn crackled laughter. "Holy shit! That's priceless! You recorded for Paulie, I hope."

"Oh, sure. But that's not even the best part."

Dawn stared, goggle-eyed. "What could be better than catching a super-rich TV evangelist on video, beating off with gummy worms in his dick?"

"It's what he was, uh, 'beating off' TO," the Writer contributed.

"What?"

"You tell her, Snowie," he said.

And then Snowie, with enthusiasm as robust as her bosom, went on to convey that Pastor Tommy Ignatius was feasting his eyes on *child pornography* whilst partaking in his most uncommon method of masturbation. Snowie even went so far as to describe in detail what was going on on the pastor's laptop screen; (however, these details will *not* be retailed to the reader; and any readers who feel short-changed by being *deprived* of these details ought to be ashamed of themselves!)

"Oh, really?" intoned Dawn. "You shouldn't have told me that because now I might have to kill that sick-in-the-head motherfucker."

"I suspect that a long and grueling end awaits our good pastor," the Writer projected, "after an extended bout of blackmail, care of Paulie Vinchetti."

Dawn chuckled. "Paulie and Augie'll do a special on him."

Snowie, on the other hand, *wasn't* chuckling. "Yeah, and *we'll* have to film it, and-and-and—"

Dawn nodded grimly. "Then we'll have to pump up Pastor Tommy's dick on the embalming machine and"—she gulped—"fuck his corpse."

The Writer paled. The conversation was getting a bit rich for him. "Snowie? Would you please reach behind the seat and get me a beer please? I'd do it myself but, well, I'm too fat and old."

Snowie all-too-happily to obliged the Writer, the effort of which caused her to lift her right buttock off of the Writer's lap for a moment, and in a fraction of that moment she slipped her hand down his pants, grabbed his genitals, jiggled her hand a few times—

"No, oh! Oh, no!"

—and triggered a massive orgasm within the confines of the Writer's pants.

"Ha, ha! I finally did it!" Snowie blared.

"Did what?" Dawn asked.

"Made him cum in his pants!" She glanced at the Writer. "Wow! You cum a lot for an old guy."

The Writer could not respond; he could only frown and gasp for breath. He frowned further when Snowie wiped her hand off on his pants.

She held up the bottle of beer (need it be elaborated that when the Writer and Dawn had picked up Snowie from her convenience store, he'd purchased a six-pack of Collier's Civil War Lager and a cooler? No, it probably needn't be mentioned.) "These aren't twist offs!" she yowled as she tried and failed to open the bottle. "Where's the opener?"

"Oh, in the name of Christopher Marlowe!" the Writer moaned. "I forgot to bring it!"

"Who's Christopher Marlowe?"

"He was the foremost Elizabethan playwright of his day—he wrote *the Tragedy of*—oh forget it! How am I gonna drink my beer?"

"What a pair of amateurs," Dawn said. She grabbed the beer, hooked the cap over her lower teeth, and pried it off with a satisfying *psst!*

After the first sip, contentment once again rested in the Writer's bosom; his own semen drying on his pants was soon forgotten. *Holmes had Watson, Jasper had Durdles, Long Ranger had Tonto. But I get these two...*

"What did Uncle Septimus say?" Dawn inquired behind the wheel. "We turn off of Tick Neck Road to Governor's Bridge?"

"I believe that's what the gentleman instructed," the Writer confirmed, yet he did not make mention of his doppelganger's allegation that Septimus Howard, the unknown son of H.P. Lovecraft, had died last night, more than likely at the hands of the newly liberated Bighead. *Do I believe that?* he asked himself. *Do I believe ANY of this?* He still wasn't sure…

"Oh, look!" Snowie said with a pleasing shudder. "Crownsville Hospital!"

The Writer looked far down a sloping field and saw the long two-story edifice of old, drab bricks. "Institutional" was the word which first came to mind, fittingly so since the building was indeed a mental institution. Double-lengths of razor-wired fences surrounded this less-than-cheery facility.

"Whole lotta fucked up people there," Dawn commented.

But the Writer thought he recalled the name from last night. "Isn't that where—"

"Yep," answered Snowie. "'Tis where the Cubbler Twins've been sittin' for all them years since they took their Ouija board up the graveyard at Crafter's house, on Halloween night, and come back to town the next mornin', pregnant as fuck!"

"Pregnant with bellies full of shit, you mean," Dawn added that delightful detail. "And look where we're going right now: the Crafter house, and I have a feeling the graveyard's on the schedule too. Why else would you have brought a shovel?"

"Well, it's true," the Writer confessed. "We have to find Crafter's grave and, well, dig him up."

"What the fuck for!?" both women yelled simultaneously.

"In due time, ladies," he said. "In due time." But now that he thought about it, he had no idea as to the purpose of this exhumation. He had only the word of his doppelganger, the implication being that once the task was accomplished, the reason for it would be obvious.

"I better not wind up with a womb full of satanic shit," Dawn said.

The Writer tightened his right arm around Snowie's waist, without conscious impulse, but it was probably to generate more contact between his crotch and her buttocks. "I'm sure that's just a local legend."

"Yeah, but what if it ain't?" Snowie fretted.

"Don't worry, Snowie. You're not going to become pregnant with feces. If that happened to anyone it would be me, because I'm the instigator." The image of such a thing was absurd yet he reflected on it anyway. His mind's eye projected it: the Writer's beer belly ballooned out times ten, pulsing with poop. "Still, it might be worthwhile to go there on some occasion, and ask to talk to them."

"They *can't* talk," Snowie reminded. "Haven't since that night up the house."

"Well, perhaps a few choice words might elicit a response and, hence, some information."

"What choice words?" Dawn asked with some skepticism.

The Writer thought of the Voynich page. "Just you leave that to me..."

The Camino roared through the road's winding curves, and the inertia caused by each curve left Snowie's backside no choice but to rock back and forth over the Writer's groin.

I better not blow another one in my pants...

"You think that's the place?" Dawn said, slowing down on the next wooded swerve.

Just as the Writer looked, he noted the ancient shotgun-peppered mailbox on whose side were the barely readable black letters: E. CRAFTER.

"Yes, Dawn," he returned. "This is indeed the place. Please pull into the entry."

In a moment's time, the vehicle sat idling at the bottom of a twisting gravel driveway and considerable incline. The Writer's eyes followed the drive up to the top of a wooded hill on which sat an extensive clearing, and in *that* sat a three-storied pile of a mansion showing only the gray of bare oak slats divested by weather and time off all traces of former paint.

"Okay, girls," he announced. "It's time we pursued our little debarkation. Dawn, please be so kind as to bring the shovel behind the seats, and, Snowie, bring that bag on the floor and—stop it! Stop it!"

The Writer's call for making this sudden vocal ejaculation was this: Snowie was deliberately jerking her buttocks back and forth over his lap, in attempts to goad something more substantial than a *vocal* ejaculation. Wincing, he tried to twist her out of his lap, but all Snowie did was buckle down harder, giggling, "Gonna make ya nut again!"

"Stop it!" the Writer bellowed. "This is silly!"

"How's this for silly?" Dawn said, looking over, and pulled her t-shirt up over her next-door-to-massive bare breasts.

The impact of this vision juxtaposed with the lewd friction of Snowie's buttocks achieved the result intended, and the Writer, for the second time in about twenty minutes, had a convulsive orgasm in his pants, and he had to admit, though embarrassed, that it was a pleasurable sensation if not a bit wild. He lay back gasping in the seat as Snowie and Dawn got out of the car, both laughing it up. The wet spot at his crotch was easily recognized, but—*Aw, so what? Nobody's going to see me up here*—and he at least contemplated a good side to this ridiculous situation. An out-of-shape, non-exercising sixty-year-old man getting off not one, but two ejaculations in twenty minutes, all without any direct stimulation to his genitals?

Not bad, he congratulated himself on the achievement.

The Writer lugged the beer up the inclined drive while the girls hauled the rest. "I feel creepy already," Snowie said, crunching over the gravel in her flip-flops.

"That's because you *are* creepy, Snowie," Dawn complimented. "You *are* creepy. Holy fuck, have you ever looked in the mirror?"

But the Writer laid down the law before Snowie could exercise her own manner of retort, with her fists. "Both of you stop right now. I'm not paying you if you fight and, Dawn, that was a mean thing to say, and you had no call to say it. If it's your time of the month, that's not Snowie's fault. Now apologize."

Dawn percolated a bit, no doubt considering that she might well lose a day's pay, which was much more than she made per day at the funeral parlor.

"Snowie, uh," she began, semi-faltering, "I'm sorry."

"Not very convincing, but good enough for now," the Writer

said. "And as punishment, *you* will dig up Crafter's grave."

Dawn crossed her arms defiantly under her superb, well, tits. "Fuck that, I did enough of that in the Army. I ain't digging no fucking grave."

"Fine," he replied, "in which case *I ain't buying you no fuckin' new car.* I'll use the extra money to buy Snowie a better car."

"I'll dig the grave!" Dawn hastily reversed her stance.

"Good. Now get up that hill, the both of you."

In spite of the Writer's new-found libidinal awareness he was happy with himself for visually examining the abundant foliage along the rising drive instead of visually examining both women's teeth-gritting rear ends. The girls, naturally, got to the top faster than he, and when he pulled up, the Writer found himself facing an eight-foot-high black iron gate secured by a stout chain and stouter padlock.

"Shit!" Snowie said.

"Yeah, shit is right. We got no tools to break that chain, and it's really dangerous climbing," Dawn pointed out the sharp rusty spikes atop the gate.

"Oh, for Telemachus' sake," the Writer complained, crestfallen. "I couldn't get over that gate even without the spikes." And, in a moment of frustration, he grabbed the lock and smacked it down against the gate.

The lock cracked open and clattered to his feet.

"Well, that's a rum thing," he commented.

"Wow." Both girls eyed him half in awe and half in wonderment. "You really is the One," Snowie said. "You shore's shit got some special *powers*."

"I don't care about special powers, Snowie," he remarked. "I just want to get in here and get the job done."

"Then I think it's about time you spilled the beans on this 'job,'" Dawn asserted. "Why are we doing this? Why on earth do you want to dig up Crafter's grave?"

The Writer smiled. "Suffice it to say, a little bird told me to."

"That's bullshit!"

"Of course it is, but it'll do for now."

They officially entered the property—a rather *desolate* property, it should be added—and the Writer felt it a fair idea to pull the gate to so that it might not be hanging open for any passersby to witness. All remained quiet as they approached the house. The Writer felt a dryness in his throat as he moved on, accompanied by a rising apprehension—the black shadow of the house seemed to stretch as if to meet him, as if to…

Welcome me back, he felt sure, and though there was no conscious recollection on his part, the Writer knew full well that he'd been to this dilapidated house sometime in the dim past. He stood still, looking up, addressing the hulking ruin with his eyes, and then he thought the most hackneyed thing: *The house knows I'm here, and unless I'm utterly mistaken, it's happy to see me.*

He dwelt not another second on this preposterous notion. Snowie held back in some inner trepidation, yet the ex-Army adventurer's spirit sent Dawn fearlessly well ahead toward the house (quite like De La Poer's unmentionable cat upon entering the twilit grotto in Lovecraft's "The Rats in the Walls." If you don't get it, you need to read that story!) More resolute details of the structure became apparent as the Writer entered the house's looming shadow and his eyes began to acclimate.

Very peculiar, came his first and most salient observation, followed by a second salient observation, or perhaps it was more akin to a feeling: that hackneyed feeling of deja vu. The hairs on his chest would've stood up if in fact he *had* any hairs on his chest. *Yeah. Absolutely no doubt. I've been here before.* It was more than his imagination, he knew. The old dilapidated pile of a house was a place he'd seen before, and with that certainty came other, even less substantial inklings.

And though the topography of the decaying edifice has little or no bearing on the narrative, a few words must be dispensed. The house stood as a narrow, three-story ruin that might be precipitously close to collapse. Of paint on the outer walls, not a vestige remained, only gray and ancient bare planks obviously hand-cut with iron froes at least three centuries ago. A front porch, if you wanted to call it that, had actually collapsed at one end, while the screens that had once enclosed it hung in tatters. The many trees around the house were gnarled, overly twisted, and appeared to be dying.

Above the wide front door was a triangular Elizabethan pediment, centered with an oculus of stained glass. The Writer's stare, next, scrutinized the building's tall, narrow sash windows (while the upper windows were of the ancient lancet style) and he found himself puzzling over the frames of the window embrasures. They...

They look too perfect for an abandoned house of this age...

But Dawn had already noticed the incongruence, and was bending over a window on the porch, tapping on the glass. The Writer had no choice but to wince in an aroused anguish since this act (in other words, the act of Dawn bending over) only served to elucidate the morphology of her backside, which a sophisticated scribe such as himself might label *recherché* or impeccable. And this observation only disheveled his ability to focus on the question at hand.

"This isn't glass," Dawn announced. "I think it's Lexan."

"The hail's Lexan?" Snowie asked, while evidently scratching her ass.

"It's *bulletproof* glass," said the Writer, "and preposterously expensive, which begs the query: why spend huge money on expensive windows for a house so dilapidated as to be essentially valueless?"

Dawn's backside elucidated its details further when she bent over harder. "And I think the window frames are stainless steel just painted over with shitty paint."

Another wave of deja vu swept the Writer's vision. *Yeah, I've been here before, over twenty years ago, and I remember this particular oddity. Crafter did this on purpose. He made the house look like a hovel on the outside so not to attract attention, when actually it was refurbished from the inside to be well-nigh impenetrable.*

Now Snowie scratched one of her buoyant breasts. Perhaps it itched. "Almost sounds like Crafter wanted the house to look like shit on purpose."

"I think you're absolutely correct, Snowie," the Writer agreed, and his touch verified the same of the front door: stainless steel in a steel frame. "It looks like an abandoned dump no thief would want to break into, when in truth, burglars couldn't break in if they tried."

This made him think of Poe's "Purloined Letter" wherein a document of paramount value was fashioned to look like garbage.

"Yes," he said aloud, more to himself than to his companions. "Crafter went to all that trouble and expense to protect something inside."

"Yeah," Dawn spoke up, "but you said we're not *going* inside. We're just digging up Crafter's grave and going home."

"No, Dawn. *We're* not digging up Crafter's grave, *you* are, remember?" The Writer's brow rose. "And I may have been a trifle hasty in my implication that we wouldn't actually enter the house."

Dawn eloquently raised an objection. "*Bull*-dick! Digging up corpses is bad enough, and now you want us to bust into a house? I'm not risking jail-time for your jive! I got a sick father at home I gotta take care of! If I'm in the joint, they'll throw him into some Medicaid shit-hole!"

"Relax, Dawn," scoffed the Writer. "What happened to the big bad rough and tumble Army girl? Have you no sense of adventure? You're not gonna go to the *joint*. Plus, it's not feasible that we'll be caught by law enforcement." He glanced to the shapely albino. "Snowie's not harping, is she? She's not afraid. Why so you?"

"Suck my dick!" Dawn barked. "Snowie's a potato-head, and I've got too much at stake anyway! Fuck this!"

Snowie, by the way, had heard nothing of the verbal exchange, so engrossed was she in, it seemed, the process of working a wedgie out of her panties.

The Writer assumed a didactic pose. "Dawn, you're forgetting something. I'm a millionaire. If by chance we *did* get caught, I'd merely rectify the problem the good old American way: I'd circumvent justice by hiring the best law firm in the state, and then we'd 'beat the rap,' as the hoodlums say."

This suggestion got Dawn thinking.

"And, like I said, I'll be buying each of you a brand-new car tomorrow as well as paying you each ten thousand dollars in cash before the day is out."

This new information generated the proper effect, sufficiently modifying Dawn's previous abstinence. "On second thought, I'm in."

The Writer paid a closer eye to the massive front door, and again felt that sinister *deja vu*. There was an oddity: an old knocker had been mounted on the door's center stile, an oval of tarnished bronze depicting a morose half-formed face. Just two eyes, no mouth, no other features. The Writer at once considered the potential literary symbol: *Man, human features eroded by a corrupt universe, leaving him speechless. The existential mask...*

Somebody farted—Snowie, no doubt, and the Writer's abstract musing blew away in the maelstrom. *Fuck. What was I thinking? Oh, yes—the door knocker.* Just as he knew he'd been here before, he knew he'd seen that knocker before, and not just here, but other places as well. He had the most unpleasant impression: that the knocker—impossible as it may have been—had been *following him* for the entirety of his adulthood. It had been *stalking him.*

But enough of these encumbering observations. He looked around, just short of being alarmed. Snowie was no longer on the porch with them. "Where the hell did Snowie go?"

The sound of a steady stream of water answered the question, and revealed her relocation to the straggly front yard.

"What a hayseed," Dawn remarked.

Snowie had pulled her pants down to her ankles and was currently squatting in order to displace the contents of her bladder. The Writer found the sight, somehow, fascinating.

Several moments passed without abatement; if anything the sound of the voiding stream grew louder and more forceful.

"What are you doing?" Dawn shouted. "Digging an irrigation ditch? Come on!"

"Cain't help it," Snowie said helplessly. "I gots a big bladder."

"Yeah, and you *gots* a big ass too, which I'm gonna be kicking *hard* in another minute if you don't get up here."

"You ain't kickin' shit, ya nut-dumpster, never have, never will. And when I'm done, I'm gonna break that fake leg off and use it like a pipe cleaner in yer fat pussy, and then I'll kick ya in yer giant ass with your *own foot.*"

Dawn prepared to physically present herself to this threat, but the Writer grabbed her with more than a little violence. "No more fighting!" he snapped, "and no more talking hostile to each other! I'm not kidding. Neither of you will get a dime out of me. I'm sick of this! And—" the Writer frowned in astonishment—"damn, Snowie, how can it possibly take that long to urinate?"

The question was never answered, and it was another two full minutes before Snowie had finished her business.

Dawn, meanwhile, returned to the matter at hand…no pun intended. Her breasts appeared even more alert when she insisted, "But I can promise you, no one's breaking down that front door without an air hammer or police door-ram."

"I won't need to break it down," the Writer said with confidence. "I'm simply going to open it." "Like you did the gate-lock?" Dawn asked dubiously. "That one looked strong but must've been old and rusted to shit. This won't be."

He grinned. "So, I'll use a key."

***

They were Tucker, Clyde, Gut, and Horace (for such readers that may need their memories refreshed). And they were called the Larkins Boys, though *boys* was hardly the correct word since they were in their forties. Each of them: blond buzz-cuts, over six foot, and well into 300s on the scale. They were identical quadruplets; they were also what a clinical psychiatrist would label "systematized sociopaths," which meant they were ingrained with extremely antisocial impulses, lacked any semblance of a "conscience," yet were intuitive and capable of recognizing the importance of organization and forethought—hence, the "systematized" element.

Now it needs to be added that each living component of this group known as the Larkins Boys had a special trait that proved of optimal benefit to the whole. Tucker, for instance, stood strong in his leadership abilities, while Clyde was a mechanic of impressive expertise. Gut was the "squire" of the foursome: always first to volunteer to take care of "dirty work" such as burying bodies, cleaning up the leakage that often companioned horrific murder, and the like. All of the brothers were incessantly loyal to one another, and they were also exclusively fearless. Likewise, on a good day, they could all of them manage a three-foot-plus "creamer" or "dick-spit."

Oh, but we've forgotten one, haven't we? The last and fourth member of the tetrad. Horace.

What might have been the especial area of proficiency of Horace?

Though less objectively intelligent than his brothers, and less attentive to details at hand, Horace very much was possessed of an admirable a creative bent, the degree of which often left his siblings in a state of sheer awe. It was Horace who had invented such brilliant activities as "Golf-Ball Jobs," "Raw Balling," "Box Jobs," "Dead-Dicking," "Cock-Gnarling," and "Nut-Ballooning." These were festive shenanigans of the highest order, (and if such colloquial terms are foreign to you, then you haven't read enough Edward Lee).

Horace's latest contribution to the field of sociopathic artistry may well have been his most sophisticated, and he called the process "Spider Masking."

An interesting moniker which sparked immediate wonder, yes?

Of course, it involved a mask, but what *manner* of mask?

Long ago, after the quadruplets' father had died of multiple organ-system failure including complete renal shutdown (stemmed from decades of chugging corn liquor), the boys had grimly entered the room of this larger-than-life man, and found a wooden locker in his closet. It was possessed of a maddeningly tenacious lock and which took the better part of a full half hour for the strapping sons to remove with several hefty crowbars.

Within were found many curious items, most of which shocked them—such as nudie magazines, but not nudie magazines hosting naked women, such as *Playboy, Penthouse,* and *Hustler* ...magazines of quite another variety: *Dune Buddies, Meat Men, Glen Swann's Cock Gobblers,* and a number of others that need not be elaborated upon via further description. This came as quite a disorienting shock to four young identical quadruplet brothers who presumed their dear dead father had been a typical backwoods pussy buster, prongin' dirty redneck poontang every chance he got, the stinkier the better, and a-fillin' their yaps with cum any chance he get, just like most fellas.

In fact, this gentleman had oft preached to his sons, "I better not never hear'a you boys ever suckin' no dick 'er takin' a hard one up the ass. Taint natrull, jess like Father Prosser at the church say ever Sunday. You ever take a dick up the ass, you're gonna get my booted foot up it not long after. Ya wanna fuck a goat or a sheep or a horse, fine, but don't'cha never, ever fuck no *fellas*, or's'll the good Lord jess might strike ya down." He pointed a commanding finger. "Any time yer pecker got shit on it, it damn well better be a *gal's* shit, ya hear?"

The boys heard, loud and clear, to be sure, and thought nothing of it afterwards…until that moment when the locker was opened and its contents divulged. "Well holy ever-livin' HAIL, Tucker! S'this mean Pa were a *homo?*" one of them asked.

"Looks that way. What else could 'splain it?"

Gut appeared in full shock: "I'se cain't believe it! *Pa? Our* Pa? Lettin' other fellas pack his fudge'n suckin' their cocks'n swallerin' their load? No!"

Clyde just shook his head with downcast eyes. "If there was ever a man in the whole world I could *never* picture with a dick in his chops, 'tis Pa. Guess he been garglin' the nut all's his life but in *secret*."

"No!" Gut wailed again. "Jess cain't be true!" and it actually looked as if he might break out in tears.

But here was where Tucker's leadership traits came into play, and he stepped up to stand in a position of control and command, a position which incited attention.

"Listen here, fellas. Ain't no reason to be all bent outta shape over this. Folks these days don't care 'bout such things any more no ways. Shee-it, I hear in California, two fellas can blow each other in *public* and no one sees no wrong in it, jess like you can smoke pot on the street and that's all okay, but, damn, don't dare light a Marlboro in the street're you'll wind up in jail. When fellas butt-fuck each other so's much they get the AIDS, they get free doctorin', a food card, and disability fer life, yes sir! They're practically *hee-roes* fer stickin' their dicks in each other. S'way folks see things these days. Modern times, ya know?" Tucker emphasized his point by pointing to his own head. "And when ya *think* about it, it makes perfect sense. What makes one man like something and another man *not* like it? The fuckin' *brain*. Take okra, fer 'zample. Plenty'a folks *love* okra but just as many say it make 'em sick. Me? Ain't no food in my sight better'n cattail pancakes, but most hill folk don't care for 'em. My favorite color be blue, but, Gut, yers is red, Clyde's is green, and Horace like orange. Why is this? 'Cos there's somethin' in my *brain* that say I like blue the best, and somethin' in Clyde's brain brain make his like green'n so on. My point? None of us gots any choice but to like what our brains *tell* us to like, and no one can say the reason fer this. I didn't *choose* ta like okra—I just up'n *do*. A fella cain't *control* what he likes'n dislikes. I cain't suddenly change my mind and say I don't like okra. Right?"

The remaining three brothers contemplated these words, then all nodded.

"So's it *has* ta be the same fer havin' a nut. The brain tells most fellas that splittails are hot to look at, and the place we wanna blow our peckersnot is right up their dirty coozes. For me, for you fellas, we'se wanna put our face in *pussy*, not some dude's hairy ass. But there's other fellas the opposite. Ain't nothin' hot to them 'bout tits and ass, they want cock'n balls, and they prefer the feel of a big *dick* up their ass to their own dicks up a gal's baby-maker. And the reason for this is…?"

"The noggin," Gut figured. "Somethin' in it make it that way, fer whatever reason."

Tucker *cracked* his big hands together with a grin. "There! See? You boys got it now. Pa didn't choose to wanna get cornholed by fellas, his *brain* decided for him. So's what we all up'n arms about? Pa was a homo." Tucker shrugged. "Big deal. Who cares? No one. What's wrong with that? Nothin'!"

More murmurs of affirmation rose from the other brothers, and suddenly the vibe in the air went from one of confusion and disbelief to one of good feelings.

Which takes us back to the original purpose of this quite

unnecessary transitional prelude: the notion of Horace's especial turn for creativity in general, and the revelation of his latest mode of fucking women all up in a big way, that being the process he'd invented called "Spider Masking."

You see, other items resided in that wooden locker besides homosexual magazines and rubber penises and butt-plugs. First, there was a piece of fancy bordered paper called a DD214 with these words on it: DISHONORABLE DISCHARGE. The second thing was a mask, a black rubber mask with straps and two big roundish windows on it—to be precise, an M17A1 gas-protective mask, compliments of the U.S. Army Chemical Corps.

As youngsters, the Larkins boys had circled round Pa many a time to listen to his tales of combat bravery and, to use his own term "airing out gooks," much the way children in olden times gathered round the fireside to listen with wonder to the aged grandam who (to use M.R. James' terms) narrated story after story of ghosts and fairies, and inspired her audience with "a pleasing terror." And Mr. Larkins had much terror to relate.

"See, boys," the man began, "back then we was locked in a battle for freedom against the commies—gooks, they was—ya know? Slopes, pan-faces, Charlie Comm, we called 'em. They was tryin' ta take over all'a southwest Asia and make folks slaves to pick rice fer the commissar. Well, as God-lovin' Americans, we wouldn't stand fer that, so's we'se fought our asses off out in the jungle, a-helpin' the people of South Viet Nam to live free, even though damn near ever-one'a them folks hated our guts, which—well, don't make much sense fer us to be fightin' for 'em then, I guess—kind of a dumbass war now that I think of it. Why risk yer life fer people that hate'cha?"

And here, Pa went off on something of a philosophical tangent. "Kind'a like Aff-ganner-stan and the Eye-Rack. We spend a couple trillion dollars helpin' those towel-head fuck faces, and lose five thousand G.I.'s, but they don' even fuckin' say thank you. They hate us more'n they hate anyone 'cos we don't believe in Mohammad or Ali or any'a them other famous boxers. Dumbest ass thing I ever heard, fightin' fer people that hate yer guts. And now we got these ISIS folks.

Cuttin' off babies' heads on account their parents ain't soooonies, the fuck whatever that is. Kind'a make ya wonder. What kind of a person could think it's a-okay to cut off a baby's head? Well, I'll tell ya what kind, boys. It be the kind'a person that *don't deserve ta live!* Fuck 'em all, I say. Let's pray our God-lovin' new president steps on all'a their dicks—fuck it, drop the big one! Show 'em who's boss! They think *they're* bad? Push the button, Mr. Prezz—BOOM! How's *that* fer bad, ya camel jockies? *Now* it's Miller Time!"

His young sons looked back with shared expressions of confusion, and one of them, a youthful Tucker, interrupted the politically incorrect rant. "Say, Pa, ya know, we don't really wanna hear 'bout *that* war. We wanna hear 'bout the one *you* was in."

"Yeah, Pa," Clyde piped up. "Did'ja kill any'a them pan-faces?"

Pa nearly choked on his next slug of moonshine. "Shee-IT, son! Did I kill *any*? I killed enough'a them evil little dinks ta fill a dozen fuckin' garbage trucks, I did. We stacked 'em up like cordwood and used 'em for fuckin' sand bags." (This phrase, by the way, was an old Army axiom, used long before Clint Eastwood). "You should'a heard 'em jabber when they'se know they're gonna die—blubberin' like babies, but—aw, no—they weren't a-blubberin' when they'se was *killin'* babies, no, sir, nor when's they was *rapin'* babies neither. 'Twas the Vee-Cee and the NVA, boys, make the Nazi SS look like the Girl Scouts. These sick bastards had *field orders*, they did, that whenevers they kill some'a our guys, they'se was supposed ta *cook* them dead bodies and then *eat* 'em, and that's no lie, boys, and *that's* what they did. Roasted our G.I.'s in a big pit, wait a full day, then have ats, stuffed their faces, they did, then next day they'd all shit in one great big pile and throw a unit patch on the pile, so when our LRRPs come out they know that all that shit used ta be our buddies. Don't read 'bout *that* in no hiss-tree books, no sir!"

Pa paused for moment of mourning, and gulped. "We should'a nuked the lot of 'em, jess like Eisenhower wanted. Turn that whole evil dink country into a smokin' hole. Then President Nixon—God bless him—he had 'em beggin' fer peace after he carpet bombed Hanoi fer nine days straight. Ah, but the shit didn't work out, then the Watergate come 'round and Nixon couldn't resume the bombing when them slopes broke the cease fire. And in the end the good ole U.S. of A. get kicked right *outta* that stinkin' shithole...

The boys continued their upward stare of wonder, mixed now with a speck of horror. One of them said, "So's...so's we *lost* the war, Pa?"

Pa's vigor for telling the story began to fade, then his eyes seemed to glow with a dark, sick-colored luminescence. "So the hiss-tree books say, but you tell me. Them pan-faced devils kilt sixty thousand of ours, but we kilt *two million'a* them."

This information certainly left an indelible impression on the four young boys. The truth, however, was a trifle different: Pa Larkins had in fact never killed anyone in Viet Nam, he'd never fired a shot, he'd never seen the enemy, and he'd never even had time to go on a mission, because not two days after arriving at Firebase Bastogne, he'd been caught by MP's performing aggressive fellatio on a fellow soldier behind the fuel depot; hence, his "combat tour" in Viet Nam was cut quite short via UCMJ criminal charges and he was transferred posthaste to the Army's Mannheim Prison in Germany. This was where he would serve the remainder of his two-year enlistment, stripped of rank, and kept active by the process of literally turning large rocks into small ones with a twenty-pound sledge hammer. You see, back in those days, men "sucking dick" or banging each other in the backside was *not allowed* in any branch of the United Stated Military. (Fortunately, these draconian laws would fade, and it would later become perfectly acceptable for soldiers to participate in these activities with gusto and zeal.)

So much for *that* story, but attentive readers are likely wondering just what *any* of the past 2,500 words has to do with the subject of this transition. In a word, nothing, but in more than a word they explain rather circuitously why the wooden locker was in Pa's long-disused closet, and why there was an Army-issue gas mask in it. Modern writers would've gotten straight to the point and relieved the reader of the burden of such superfluous wordage. Ah, but how different might the tenets be of a novelist into whose aesthetic philosophy the beams of economical prosecraft have not yet penetrated!

We'd been discussing the especial individual proficiencies of each of the four brothers, and had learned that Horace had an instinctive aptitude for creativity, and that his recollection of Pa's old gas mask played a notable part of it.

You see, far more so than his brothers, Horace was bored and even offended by merely raping and killing bad women—"bad" meaning women who stole or sold drugs or otherwise engaged themselves as haughty bitches within the limits of the grand town of Luntville. Women, in other words, who had it coming, or simply weren't fit to exist among good people. Like that druggie-cunt they'd long-necked the other day, or that other one this morning they'd brain-joggled by clamping her head into the paint-shaker machine at the hardware store. (Yes, sir! They'd turned her into a jabbering retard a mite quick, and each hammered out a piece of her ass right there on the floor, just a little while before that Writer fella had walked in and got himself a shovel!)

But Horace did not sit long on his laurels after initiating such brilliant and original processes with which to, uh, to *fuck women up*. His creative drive caused him to get right back to work, using his brain to devise *the next* mode of "rucking" (the word "rucking" being the backwoods parlance for, well, fucking women up). And here was where that gas mask came in.

See, next to Mayor Eamon's big barn where they all did most'a their rucking, there also stood several disused tool sheds (which might remind sharper readers of Lovecraft's "The Dunwich Horror," however, no cosmic monsters would be found therein). Now, even the most ignorant rednecks become, via parental word of mouth, well apprised of the natural hazards that exist in their proximity. Copperhead snakes, for instance, slithered in abundance through these woods, and so too did timber rattlesnakes. Wild and often rabid—dogs were not scarce, and it was not unheard of for bears to rear their heads in the wilds about Luntville. And we mustn't forget a vast array of ticks, most of which were chock full of Lyme Disease and Rocky Mountain Spotted Fever. Unseen sinkholes pitted the woods and marshlands like minefields, and a few unlucky wanderers had even been lost in quicksand. And last but not least, we find perhaps the most unique inconvenience of all in this grand and beautiful state.

That would be an arachnid of the genus *Loxosceles,* also known more famously as the Brown Recluse spider. This little beast, no bigger than a quarter, serves as the bane of many a rural and woodland town, and though their bite is rarely deadly, the venom possesses a diabolical constituent named *sphingomyelinase D*, which functions as an aggressive dermo-necrotic agent, a molecular compound that causes all flesh around the bite to die and then rot, forming a crater which often never heals and corrodes the flesh down to the bone.

So, it's no overstatement to say that this minuscule spider is one motherfuckin' *tough* customer, and Horace practiced upon his knowledge of them and their possibilities. (He'd even been bitten by a Brown Recluse as a child and still had the hole in his calf to prove it!) Anyway, the long and short of it (well, mainly the *long* of it) is this: Horace not too long ago had gone into that previously mentioned toolshed next to the mayor's barn; he'd needed a wood plane because he'd wanted at the time to shear off the inverted belly button of a pregnant hill girl who'd been caught siphoning gas. But his search for the tool hadn't lasted long; in fact he'd barely set foot in the shed when a spider web had spread across his very big face, and in the corner of his eye, backed by more than a little terror, he'd glimpsed a little spider scampering across his eye socket.

Horace was no wussy, and he could duke it out with the best of them. But *spiders?*

Fuck that.

He tried to swat the revolting thing off, opening his mouth to wail, but—wouldn't you know it?

The spider scrabbled craftily into Horace's mouth.

This made him insensible; he stumbled backwards, nearly blacking out, and fell out of the teetering shed, landing hard on his immense back. At the moment of impact, some mindless impulse caused him to expectorate. When he regained some semblance of consciousness, a probe of his tongue convinced him that no spider remained in his mouth.

On the ground next to him, there sat his plop of spit, and in its viscid confines the spider struggled, still alive. Horace's hillbilly indoctrination revealed to him at once that the occupant of the spit was indeed a Brown Recluse spider; this was easily discerned by the violin-like marking on the thorax. "Fuck me!" Horace exclaimed. "A real live Brown *Ree-cloose* spider went right inta my pie hole!"

Talk about a close-call. He stepped on the wicked thing and then with painstaking care nudged back into the shed and shined his flashlight around. It was an awesome yet gut-shimmying sight.

The entirety of the shed's interior was *festooned* with Brown Recluse webs loaded with egg-sacs. It was a *jungle* of webs in there, and the ceiling, the webs, the walls, were *teeming* with movement: eggs hatching fifty at a time, hatchlings and juveniles and adults *everywhere. Thousands* of them, all afrolic in their Spider Paradise.

Fuck this! Horace closed the door, then put a sign on it: OFF LIMMITS! SPIDDERS!

Of course, the wood plane was never procured, so first he and his brothers, along with Mayor Eamon, tended to the pregnant girl with a different tool: their trusted all-purpose tin-snips, with which they cut off her ears, lips, and nipples. Killing her was not in true order because they all firmly believed that the punishment must suit the crime, which suggested that the Larkins boys maintained a considerable respect for fairness. Be that as it may, when the pregnant girl limped away, now half-insane, she was one hurtin' pup, and you can be sure, she would never steal gas again!

Oh, and upon her release...she wasn't pregnant anymore. Tucker's big hickory ax-handle had taken care of that, ("Batter up!") and the mayor had applauded this maneuver, stating, "Good job, son. Ya done up'n saved the taxpayers another food card." (Readers with a particularly morbid bent will want to know what exactly was done with the miscarried fetus, but I'm afraid I'm not possessed of the information required to inform you on that note.)

Anyway...

After discovering the hive of Brown Recluse spiders in the toolshed, Horace's creative flair got to spinning its gears. First, he went to Worden's Hardware store on Main Street and there appropriated a pack of Catchmaster Pro Sticky Traps made especially for Brown Recluse spiders. These were small cardboard "tents" with adhesive bottoms. The adhesive contained a chemical scent that attracted spiders like the scent of fresh meat attracted pit bulls. The spiders took the bait, got stuck on the "floor" of the trap, and that was that. Of course it wouldn't serve Horace's *leit motif* to have a shitload of Brown Recluses stuck on a trap; therefore, and with his usual ingenuity, he encased the traps in plastic screen. This allowed the scent to escape but when the spiders came for the bait, they couldn't get caught in the trap.

Pretty smart, yes?

By now, the frowning reader, weary of hoeing through all these unnecessary words, is likely asking him-or-herself, *What the FUCK does all this have to do with an old Vietnam-era gas mask?*

The answer, at last, is within reach!

Horace—his Thinking Cap buzzing away—retrieved the gas mask from the wooden locker full of homosexual magazines and rubber phalli, placed several traps inside it, and then, very carefully and very quickly, opened the shed door, slid the mask inside, and re-closed the door. Then he chugged himself a beer (Icehouse, for those who wanted to know, the King of Redneck Beers, next to Milwaukee's Best, of course) and then went on the hunt for the next component of his idea: a good ole all American "splittail" aka "jizz-bucket" aka "woman."

Such types were not difficult to come by in these parts, and it just so happened that the Larkins boys enjoyed a very positive acquaintanceship with local boot-legger Clyde Nayle. Mr. Nayle, on quite a regular basis, caught creeker girls trying to rip off an ear or two of his corn, and whenever he did, he'd whup the shit out of the poor creature, lay down some heavy peter, and lock her up in a chicken pen. He'd keep them in the pens at least two weeks and give them only a cup of water per day (food was out of the question; these girls had to learn that stealing was bad). The gals were rack-skinny to begin with, so you can bet they were a mite skinnier when he finally let them go. He'd starve them down to seventy or so pounds—yes, sir! *Good* and skinny!

In fact, one time, the good Mr. Nayle had forgotten he'd had one in the pen and by the time he'd remembered, the starvation had whittled her down to less then *fifty* pounds, just a pile of twitching bones and skull covered with paste-white skin. He'd let her go in the woods but all she could do was crawl a little and, well, she hadn't made it far before the animals had gotten to her.

But, guess what? That girl *never stole corn* again!

However, for the sake of completeness, we must include a word or so about Nayle's sixteen-year-old son, Tater (lots of rednecks named their sons Tater, by the way, and Dumar and Luke). Tater was a bit sick in the head from the get-go, and whenever his daddy had some girls in the pens, the young man was never at a loss for entertainment. One of his favorite ploys was wiping his ass with a big beautiful ear of white corn and putting it in the pen, and you can rest assured that the girl ate it lickety-split. He also liked to beat off on Saltines or blow his nose or hock a big lunger on a slice of bread. Do you think these girls ate it?

Oh, they ate it, all right.

But the best Tater Tale is thus: the fine young man had squatted right in front of a pen in whose confines lay a splittail that had been shrinking away in there for near two weeks. See, Tater had brought with him a big-ass pulled pork sandwich on a paper plate. He picked it up, was about to take a bite, but stopped, saying, "Aw, shee-it. I'se sorry, hun. Pretty dang rude'a me ta sit here an' eat this sammitch without offerin' you some, huh?" The sunken-eyed girl began to mewl, and rattle around in the pen. "So here's what I'll do fer ya, me bein' a nice guy'n all. You'n me? We make a deal, okay? You drink my piss, and I'll give you half'a this sammitch. How's that sound?"

The girl mulled the maleficent offer around in her mind for all of one second and cranked open her mouth full of loose teeth. *I guess that's a yes!* Tater stood up, whipped it out, and peed a hard steady steam into her agape maw. It was a considerable urinary void, and the girl, like a trooper, gulped and gulped and gulped, and swallowed a commendable volume. But then, Tater seemed to recollect himself, and after putting his dick back in his pants, said, "Dang, forgot somethin', sweetie," and he disappeared only to return a moment later, bearing *another* paper plate. "Let's face it, hun. Drinkin' some pee ain't that big a deal when ya git right down to it. So we'se'll up the ante. I'll give you the *whole* sammitch if'n you eat this first," and then he lowered the paper plate to the slot in the pen.

This plate differed from the first one, in that there was no sandwich on it. Instead, it hosted a fair portion of fairly fresh excrement.

"This here's a pile of shit," Tater stated the obvious. "Eat *that*, and the sammitch is yours."

The girl's face twisted up into a rictus of outrage, and she *howled*.

"Aw, but set'cher heart at ease," Tater continued. "That ain't *my* shit, oh, no. I wouldn't do *that* to ya! It ain't nothin' but a little possum shit."

The girl's howl trebled in intensity, and she was actually crying like a baby as well.

"It'd be a damn shame if all ya come away with outta this is a belly full'a hot piss," the boy remarked, "but now, I admire ya fer havin' the self-respect not ta do it. Oh, what the hail, lemme give ya a taste so's ya know what you'll be missin' if ya decide not to."

He took a good-sized pinch of that juicy pulled-pork from the edge of the sandwich. The girl's open mouth was already in wait, pressed against the pen wire, and into it, Tater daintily released the pinch of delectable meat onto the girl's tongue, whereupon, she sucked it in and squealed in a delight much more clarified than orgasm; she moaned and mewled and crooned, hugging her knees and rocking back and forth with tears in her eyes.

"Aw, now, hun, no waterworks—that makes me feel bad," Tater said. "But that is some good pig, ain't it? Now, my daddy can *make* some barbecue, and I see how's you'a jest sittin' in there, gettin' skinnier'n skinnier ever day, and I'd *love* ta wartch you eat that whole juicy big-ass sammitch, and I know how much ya'd enjoy it. But a'course, you gots a decision ta make, and ya better make it quick, less'n I eat it myself."

If ever a facial expression could simultaneously manifest sheer, undiluted hatred and sheer, undiluted despair, it was the look on that starving creek woman's visage at that moment.

Some kind of awful, sickening static seemed to seep through the air, a power that some might call malignant or even *Tartarean*—a vibe or frequency or something less explicable that would make a sane person's hairs stand on end.

There may as well have been a drum roll, then, when the emaciated hill girl picked up the paper place, brought its contents to her cracked lips, and sucked that glossy turd into her mouth, chewed it, and swallowed it.

Now, not even a writer such as Lovecraft, Poe, or Baudelaire could harness the proper words that would accurately describe the expression on her face as she looked back at Tater.

"Well good gawd-*dang*, girl!" the boy celebrated. "That is what *I'se* talkin' about! You is one tough chick! And now, jess like I promised, I'se gonna give you that sammitch! Take it, it's all yours!"

And then Tater walked away, leaving the sandwich at an inaccessible distance from the slot at the bottom of the pen.

For the next hour, the girl wailed and screamed her protestations at the outrage perpetrated upon her, convulsing, biting at the pen wire till her front teeth broke, and yanking on those wires till they cut through to the bones of her fingers. And for the remainder of that day and into the early evening, she lay nearly comatose on her side and watched a variety of rats and field mice and what not make raids on the succulent sandwich. Round about sundown, something none other than a possum waddled out and finished the sandwich off right in front of the girl. Wouldn't it be ironic if it were the same possum whose feces now occupied her stomach?

But I'm sorry to say that the tale's bleakness does not end here, for upon first light, Clyde Nayle loped out to the pen to give the girl one last fucking and then let her go but, lo, this would not come to be. The poor girl had died during the night, infected by some manner of disease—E. Coli or Salmonella or some such—that had no doubt taken up habitation in the possum feces, and by the time

Mr. Nayle got to her, most of her digestive system had liquified and exited her anus...

Oh, dear. How I *do* stray off sometimes! Where was I? Oh, yeah, the gas mask...

Horace Larkins had all the pieces in place to make his new idea a sure-fire winner, but he needed a test run, so to speak, and for this, of course, he needed a *victim,* namely a victim of the female variety and one whose bearing in life warranted punishment. Therefore, he prevailed upon the boot-legger Mr. Nayle to address this requirement, and Mr. Nayle was all too happy to oblige any of the Larkins brothers, so genuine was their friendship.

Like a dealer on a car lot, Mr. Nayle escorted Horace to the pens to show the visitor his current inventory. Four mewling, skinny, and very unhappy nude women occupied the pens. "There they is," said Mr. Nayle with a certain tone of pride. "Take your pick." Horace took stock of the skeletal collection, and he did so with some scrutiny, but they were all quite similar: just dirty, huge-eyed hill girls with sucked-in cheeks and ribs showing, whose only crime was trying to pilfer an ear of corn. One, it seemed, was as good as another.

Clyde Nayle indicted the pen's only blonde, and remarked, "This 'un here still got some tits on her and she don't put up any fuss when yer a-fuckin' her, but a'course they'se all quite used ta havin' a dick stuck in 'em from their fathers'n brothers, I imagine. And this 'un here"—he indicated an upper pen which provided the domicile for a greasy-haired brunette— "this 'un here's a good blowjob on account she had no teeth 'cept fer three front ones, so's I yanked 'em out with the pliers. She swallers all the nuts too, like all creekers, on account she like it and 'tis a free meal."

But Horace seemed strongly in favor of the last girl, skinny and dirty as the others but seemingly still possessed of some vestige of prettiness about the face. "Purdy face, here," Horace commented.

Mr. Nayle nodded in concurrence. "Oh, yeah, a right purdy she is. 'Twas fixin' ta ugly that face up a bit afore's I let her go but seein' how's you like her, you kin have her."

"Well, thanks much, Clyde!" Horace expressed. "That's a right nice of ya!"

"Anything fer my fine neighbors the Larkins brothers," Mr. Nayle said with genuineness.

But Horace paused for a consideration. "I'll be uglying her up somethin' fierce," he said, "so, uh, you might not want her back when I'se done."

Mr. Nayle chuckled, "Aw, don't'cha worry 'bout that none. These stink-bags is a dime'a dozen. You'se kin bury her alive when you're done fer all I care. Here, lemme help ya git her out," and then Mr. Nayle unlocked the pen, hauled the girl out hard by her hair, and smacked her senseless with his big palm. "The bitch still got some zing in her so's lemme make shore she don't try ta run off on ya." Mr. Nayle, no stranger to effectively disabling helpless women, clipped both of her Achilles tendons with wire-cutters and he did so in a very expeditious fashion; the girl scarcely had time to yelp.

"That's dang nice of ya, Clyde," Horace said, impressed, and then he offered Mr. Nayle a $10 bill. "Here, lemme give ya some scratch fer yer trouble."

"Nope. Won't hear of it. Yer money's no good here, what with all the protectin' the community that you'n yer fine brothers do."

"Well, that's just peachy!" and then Horace began to drag the girl away—by her hair, of course. "Now, you'n your boy, just you stop by our place this Saturday 'cos me'n my brothers is havin a fish fry!"

"Will do," Mr. Nayle said, smiling and waving.

So. Now Horace had the final piece of his new idea's machinery, and it wasn't long before he'd arrived back at the toolshed with his new "splittail."

By now, the dutiful reader will have already figured what this whole gas-mask-spider thing was all about, yes? The shock-eyed and very stupefied woman lay shuddering in the dirt, while Horace pulled on his long-sleeved work gloves and then, with great care and slowness, opened the shed door and slid out the gas mask. Sure enough, the thin, screen-wrapped bait traps inside the mask were *covered* with Brown Recluse spiders, and keeping a watchful eye out for "strays," he slapped that mask over the girl's unsuspecting face and strapped it down tight.

Finally, the task was complete.

A few strays did indeed escape the mask before it was secured, but these were easily dispatched by Horace's gloved fingertips, and next he found that his previous shenanigans had left him so cringingly aroused that his pants were down and he was enjoying some very primitive intercourse within a minute. *For some reason,* he thought, *it feels so much better ta fuck a gal while she's having the holy ever-livin' SHIT tortured out of her than it does just a reg-lar gal. Don't know why, just does!*

And tortured she was, very much so, and she was copulated with hard and fast, with Horace *smacking* the gas mask every stroke. This was for a functional purpose—you see, the Brown Recluse spider would not ordinarily bite unless agitated; therefore, Horace gave it his best effort to *agitate the fuck out of them*. The typical adult Brown Recluse could bite multiple times before depleting its venom, and even then it would replenish quickly.

It should go without saying (but it *will* be said anyway) that that mask-ful of spiders began biting right away, and you can reason that the girl began *screaming* right away from the incognizable pain, and of course, this screaming only agitated the spiders further: a macabre cycle of terror, agony, agitation, then more terror and agony. As the process went on, the muffled screams seemed to lose the characteristics that associated them with that of the human voice; soon these vociferations ground down to belching, blurting, grating sounds much like when you're trying to start a car with a bad flywheel.

Eventually, Horace's "nut" arrived, and his semen was dispersed liberally into the nameless girl's appalled vagina. Still safe in his long gloves, then, he slowly removed the mask, flung it back into the shed and slammed the door, and squashed the few spiders that had gotten on his gloves. As for the quivering victim, the several strays that remained on her face, once in direct sunlight, "headed for the hills," so to speak, making haste for the nearby woods. At this point, Horace took a long, close look at her.

Now, make no mistake. Horace's orgasm had been an especial treat, but not nearly the treat that his first glimpse of the victim's face proved to be.

Just now, the face looked like a cranberry pie with most of the crust picked off. Via the efficacy of the spiders, her once pretty visage now was just a blue-maroon mass of glistening bumps. The swelling fully obfuscated the lips, nose, and eyes—it was a most unique sight—and that she lay there shuddering made it even better, for that meant she was still alive, and Horace *wanted* her alive.

You see, his fantasy was to have a "skull-faced" girl to fuck. The venom had necrotized the flesh on her face, and then the face would quickly turn gangrenous and then rot away down to the bone. This sounded cool, to Horace, and after he and his brothers had had enough of fucking her, he'd let her go right nearby her little creeker village. He could imagine the look on all those hillbilly faces when she walked into the camp with *that* face!

So, at last, the deed was done, and Horace couldn't wait to observe the various stages of decomposition that the face would undergo over the next few days. His dick got hard again just thinking about it, and harder still when considering how awed his brothers and the Mayor would be when they witnessed his latest work of genius!

Then Horace dragged her (by the hair, of course) into the big barn and locked a big iron collar around her neck, which was chained close to the wall right next to the special metal chair Horace had built for "long-neckin" chicks, and you can bet, that was a *whole* lot of fun!

Now that he'd done his good deed for the day, he looked at his watchless wrist, thought, *Dang! I thank it's time fer a beer!* and loped right to the fridge that the Mayor kept here precisely for that reason. Ah, but as luck would have it—

Shucks!

—there was absolutely no beer to be found. *My alker-hollic brothers must'a drinked it all...* But patience was a virtue, so went the saying, and Horace had a fair amount of patience. Whistling that great old tune "Sixteen Tons," by Tennessee Ernie Ford, he moseyed down to the creek where they stockpiled multiple cases of Icehouse cans in the cool rushing water so it wouldn't get skunky when the fridge was full.

Well he cracked open one of those bad boys right away and

downed a third of it, and smacked his lips at the chilled satisfaction of the processed, shit-tasting mass-market domestic slop that rednecks loved only because it had extra alcohol injected into it, and then he thought, *What a gosh durn fine day I'm'a havin', yes sir! Thank you, God!*

God was, to no surprise, not particularly interested in Horace's displays of gratitude, but that is neither here nor there. What is pertinent, though, is this announcement, which is what might be thought of as a wincing narrative break or, sort of, the inept narrator "breaking" the Fourth Wall (something he is known to do quite a bit of late, probably because he's getting old as fuck) by changing the limited third-person viewpoint of this character *in the midst of the same transition,* which is something competent writers NEVER do.

But fuck it.

This is an ill-proportioned tale anyway, and that makes it more fun, right?

Right?

Back to the point. Earlier I used the famous quote, "patience is a virtue," and by now, you readers have demonstrated yourselves to a virtuous lot, indeed. (Wait, now I'm curious; who coined that phrase, "patience is a Virtue?" Let me check...Ah, I see, it was first invented in 1360 by someone named William Langland. Hmm. Never heard of him.)

But this is a sequel to the sequel of Edward Lee's mid-'90s novel *The Bighead,* yet we've scarcely caught a glimpse of the monster yet, just one brief transition thrown in as an afterthought. Well, I'm happy to inform you that *things are about to change.*

Back at the Crafter House, the "Writer" and his two well-bosomed and not so well-bred sidekicks were trying to conceive of a way to open the ornate front door, and just as said Writer cast a glance toward the distant woodlands and thought yet again *If the Bighead is actually real, which I suppose it is, because I SAW IT, then...where is it?* our friend Horace had just finished his first can of Icehouse, squashed the can and chucked it, and prepared to retrieve another, he—Horace, not the Writer—was reciting some lines from that great old Ford song, "Sixteen tons of Number Nine coal, the supervisor said 'Well, bless my soul,'" when he heard a stout crunching sound behind him.

He figured his brothers must've returned from their outing, and this prospect excited him mightily. He procured another beer from the cool water, blurted, "Hey, fellas, just wait'll you see what I done to a splittail I got me from one'a Clyde Nayle's chicken pens—shee-it! Just wait!" but then his enthusiasm dwindled, for the reflection of his visitor in the rushing stream by no means resembled any of his brothers, and a sudden stench rushed up and gagged him: a stench akin to sweaty ass-crack or, well, something exponentially worse; in fact, so dense was this stench that Horace's eyes smarted. Then he spun round, to find out what this was all about.

No perplexity crossed his mind in the few seconds of cognizance he had left, nor did ever a question come to mind: he knew for fact that he was facing horrifying local legend, facing it in the flesh.

Facing the Bighead.

Of course, he'd never believed the stories. Monsters didn't really exist. They were just things that parents made up to scare their pain-in-the-ass kids. But now that conviction had been supremely nullified, for nonexistent monsters didn't stink like the bottom of a garbage truck in high summer, and neither did nonexistent monsters grab big 350-pound redneck men by their belts, hoist them in the air, spin them around, and then haul their pants off, all in essentially one swift and controlled motion.

A bunch of ribs cracked then, as Horace was flung to the ground by this Legend-in-the-Flesh, this eight-foot-tall monstrosity with a head the size of a toilet, yellow, brown-splotched skin tacky skin, and a foot-long-plus flap of foul meat dangling at its groin over a pair of testicles the size of Florida avocados, not the smaller California ones. A huge hand that was in no way human reached down and—WHAM!—yanked off Horace's own cock and balls, and then Horace was junkless, shuddering, and peeing through a urethra no longer connected to a penis.

Alas, poor Horace had had his last "nut." He didn't scream or shriek or yell from the incognizable pain; in fact, the assault had occurred so quickly, Horace's nervous system pretty much shut down from the shock. If any coherent thoughts at all occupied his mind now, they were simply thoughts of a hasty death. How could he possibly live without genitals? No more dandy orgasms, no more "rucking," and no more fucking up gals. Why bother living?

Anyway, Horace wouldn't have to worry about living half a minute later, because the Bighead spat on the thumb of its right hand (which was about the size of one of those eight-ounce Oscar Meyer liverwursts you could get in grocery stores), and in no time, that monster-thumb had disappeared right up Horace's ass, and via this new connection, Horace was lifted from the ground, groin spurting blood, and then the Bighead's left hand seized his captive's by jaw, and what happened then was, well, pretty cool.

See, the monster's thumb up Horace's ass effectively sealed off this celebrated excretory orifice, and now the monster's morass of a mouth sealed its lips over Horace's nose and mouth, and then—you guessed it—exhaled long and hard into Horace's body. After a few more exhalations, the fat captive's belly bloated and bloated until it looked like the belly of an Alderney cow that had died in the field and whose belly swelled to gigantic proportions from so much putrefactive gas.

It proved a spectacular sight, and even more spectacular it was when the Bighead released one more exhalation into Horace's aghast mouth and his entire abdomen ruptured with a great, cracking *POP!* and I can't even describe the nature of what jettisoned from the meaty rent, save to say that it was a fascinating expulsion.

Well, so much for the tale of the gas mask.

The Bighead pulled a can of beer from the water, noticed the pop-top thing on it, figured it out immediately (just because he was a deformed hybrid didn't mean he was stupid), and opened the can with a little *pzzzt!* He'd seen the fat redneck man drinking from a similar can so Bighead decided to do the same. He sucked the can's entire contents into his mouth, prepared to swallow, but upon actually *tasting* the dreck, spat it out in a great plume and grimaced. It tasted so awful that he had to suck the shit off his thumb to get that Icehouse taste out of his mouth.

***

If the Bighead is actually real, the Writer was thinking, *which I suppose it is, because I SAW IT, then...where is it?* He made this rumination while standing on the Crafter front porch, looking down the hill into dense woods. *That's where it'd be. In the woods.*

This thoughtful delay of a segue was caused in part by a brief interruption in which Dawn had gone back to the shiny white El Camino after some further conversation about the door.

She had frowned acutely at his boastful assertion. "You have a key to the fuckin' Crafter House?"

The Writer's grin had maintained its intensity. "I have a key, in essence, to *any* house." Taking the plastic Safeway bag, he'd extricated the mummified hand. "The Hand of Glory, remember? The left hand of a hanged murderer, cut off while its owner's neck was still in the noose. It's a totem of age-old occult science and when used by a faithful practitioner, it will open any lock."

Dawn's awesome breasts, then, jogged magnificently as she erupted into copious, uproarious laughter.

The Writer refused to be thwarted, for he knew he must have faith in this supernatural device. But as he'd turned for the front door—

"Oh, buggery! I need a match or a lighter, and I don't have either!"

Dawn, her spell of laughter subsiding, snapped her fingers. "Got you covered; I left mine in the car."

"I didn't know you smoked."

"Not cigarettes, but I smoke fuckin' pot like a motherfuckin' Grateful Dead convention."

And so, back to the El Camino she'd gone, returning, tits joggling, moments later with a trusty Bic lighter. Thus bringing our narrative up to the present again and allowing events to proceed apace.

"Ah, excellent, superb, and quite the serendipity," the Writer declared.

Meanwhile, Snowie—having finally rejoined them—was holding and regarding the Hand of Glory with not so much revulsion as fascination.

"A Hand of Glory has always been a favorite witch's and warlock's tool, ever since the Dark Ages," the Writer said, feeling obliged to tout his useless knowledge. "Occultists would sneak to the gallows the night after a hanging, and remove the left hand of the executed person, usually a murderer, rapist, or heretic, and they'd cut it off with his or her head still in the noose."

"Cool!" Snowie exclaimed.

Dawn frowned. Her awesome breasts were now damp with perspiration, which made for a welcome vision as they pushed against the t-shirt. Her question addressed the Writer. "And a smart guy like you really believes that it can open that locked door?"

The Writer's mouth opened, but stalled. *Do I really believe that? The doppelganger had gotten into his room with it, right? Faith is power,* he thought. *And belief is the right hand of faith...*

"Yes, I do, Dawn. I *believe* it. Therefore it shall be."

Dawn grinned. "Yeah? Well, get on with it! This I gotta see."

Oh, ye of little faith... The Writer took the Bic lighter. Then he took the Hand of Glory from Snowie.

Then there was silence.

The Writer, in a manner as if to generate suspense, flicked the lighter, and brought the flame to each fingertip of the withered hand. Which, in turn, ignited. How this was possible, the Writer could not theorize. But—quite in defiance of the laws of physics—each finger-end burned in the manner of a candle.

Impossible.

Yet, it was so.

Nonetheless, Dawn remained amused. "I'll tell you what. If that ridiculous chopped-off hand makes the front door open, I'll suck your dick right here and now."

Ordinarily, the Writer would've frowned at so uncouth and tactless a remark but for some reason, at just that moment, hearing those words pass her lips—"I'll suck your dick"—popped a near full erection in his pants. *Fuck. More libidiny. Spending time with these girls is turning my brain into a sexual sewer...*

"But if the door *doesn't* open," Dawn continued, "then you give me a hundred bucks."

He looked her right in the eye. "You've got a deal," and then he approached the solid-steel front door with the stiffened Hand of Glory raised in his own hand the way King Solomon raised his scepter. "In the name of God, the defender of Heaven and Earth and of all things seen and unseen, I now command all unclean spirits to open this door, so be it mote."

Then he turned the doorknob, and pushed.

"Fuck!" he blurted, infuriated. "The motherfucker's still locked!"

Dawn's tits jiggled grandly as she was consumed by another burst of laughter. "Hand of Glory, huh? Is that a butt-crack I see forming in the middle of your face?"

The Writer's face reddened—he felt a perfect ass. Flustered, he squinted, and thought: *Belief, the most powerful force in existence. I must BELIEVE that this will work. I must BELIEVE that my doppelganger used it successfully last night to allow for the Bighead's re-emergence into the world. If I don't BELIEVE that, then this expedition is all for naught, and this hand is nothing more than that: a hand.*

It was not easy to concentrate in juxtaposition with Dawn's now-hyena-like-laughter. A nearly overwhelming temptation seized him, to turn and lob the accursed useless thing like a grenade, heave it into the yard.

Yet the Writer persevered, closing his eyes and thinking thus:

I BELIEVE...

At this spark of synaptic activity, seemingly of its own accord—

click

— there was a metallic click.

"Holy fuck!" Snowie squealed. "Look!"

All eyes turned to the massive front door, which now stood ajar. Dawn stopped laughing.

The Writer smiled, looking more at the plump nipples sticking out beneath the fabric of her t-shirt than at her face.

"I guess, I guess this ain't all a bunch of bullshit after all," she uttered.

"Forsooth," he replied.

"Huh?"

Snowie bubbled her own laughter. "Oh, good! Get on your

knees, sugar!" she squealed to Dawn. "You got some suckin' ta do!"

But the Writer only turned his gaze to the door. *I KNOW it was locked a few seconds ago. Yet now...* The conclusion had some interesting possibilities. *Who knows? Maybe I'm really a metaphysician!* His hand bid the open door. "Ladies first."

"No, no, not yet!" Snowie said. "I wanna see Dawn suck your dick, like she promised!" At that, Dawn began actually lowering herself to her knees.

"There'll be no dick-sucking," he said. "We're not here for that. We're here for a preternatural and perhaps even a cosmological reason."

"Huh? Cosmetics?"

"Never mind. But like I said, ladies first."

Dawn huffed. "You can lick my fuckin' ass crack! I'm not gonna be the first person to walk into this haunted house in shit knows how many years."

"Me, either," Snowie said. "But...how 'bout if I lick *your* ass crack for, like, twenty bucks?"

"Stop being silly," the Writer suggested. "We're not here for fun and games, we're here for a *reason,* a *serious* reason. But, what's that you said? The house is *haunted?* I thought it was cursed but no one said anything about haunted."

"It's haunted as fuck," Snowie said. "Tons of people have come up here and saw ghosts...I mean, at least the ones who lived to tell about it. Stands ta reason, don't it? Crafter *sacrificed* girls up here, for his satanic magic stuff."

"His necromancy," the Writer corrected.

"Whatever. And it go back long afore Crafter was even *born.* There *always* been evil fucked-up people livin' here, doin' evil fucked-up shit ta folks, all in the name'a the *devil.* So's you kin bet'cher big city-man brain that this place is haunted by ghosts, demons, and all kind'a other bad shit. How else the Cubbler twins get knocked up with shit from hell?"

It was a reasonable question, and it was anything but pleasant to picture the act which led to the conception. But true or false, this folklore only stirred Writer's interest further. *Here goes...*

He stepped into the house.

A hot and very musty environment greeted him, which was to be expected. He set the Hand of Glory down on a scroll-footed table next to the door that looked 1800s-ish; from Crafter, an antiquary, the Writer would expect that. *Gotta get some light in here, see what we got,* and with his nerdy pocket penlight, he shuffled his feet over what felt like carpet and made his way to the swags of the first window (in olden days they were called swags, not drapes—in case you didn't know that) and yanked them down with some force, which actually broke the rod, but it wasn't like Crafter could object, could he? This act of vandalism, for it could be called nothing less, released decades of dust into the air, from which the Writer urgently backed away, coughing. But at least, now, he had enough light to see, and this he used first to take down the other swags. More dust billowed, so he fled back outside to the porch while it settled.

He looked around but saw no trace of Snowie or Dawn. *Probably off smoking pot somewhere, or...* Why bothering finishing the surmise? But this was not an ideal place for two girls to go wandering off. Cursed ground, a haunted property, and there was even a witches' graveyard here, if the legends could be trusted.

A regular pair of idiots...

Another minute or two of fixing the view of the distant woodlands into his head, and he re-entered the house. Now sufficiently lit, the front parlor's details were easily revealed, and were it not festooned by cobwebs, it would've passed for the parlor of an eighteenth-century baron. Ornately framed portraits, Georgian-era furniture, gilt mirrors, and crystal chandeliers were rife, and most writers would be enthused to describe it all in precise detail; however, *this* writer will do no such thing, instead electing to leave such visualizations to the reader's imagination.

Ah. What have we here? It was impossible for our protagonist not to at once be drawn to one wall lined with books, and after a quick visual survey, the nature of the bindings and the toolwork on the leather suggested that most or all volumes present were printed before 1900. Here was an 1870 edition of *Der Hexenhammer,* translated to German by Johann Wilhelm Schmidt. Next was the famed *Daemonolatreiae libri tres* of Nicholas Remy, Lyons, 1595, and in surprisingly fine condition. A first printing of Spence's *Compendium of Demonology* and an interesting blue-leather bound *Book of Common Prayer,* printed in London in 1653. What made this "interesting" was that the Writer's recollection of marginalia reminded him that the printing of this book in 1653 was howlingly illegal, that being during Oliver Cromwell's Puritan upheaval of the English government. *The printer would probably have his head chopped off,* the Writer realized. *Crafter certainly had a taste for exceptionally rare books...*

But here was a narrow volume the Writer did not recognize, *Pronouncements of ye Glory of God & Ye Presence of Satan & his Imps & Blasphemies of an Infernall Traine of Daemons* by the Reverend Abijah Hoadley of New Dunnich in the Commonwealth of Massachusetts, printed in Springfield, 1747. This looked like meaty reading indeed, yet the Writer had no time for it now. He slipped the book back in its slot, only then noticing the volume next to it. He smiled with pride: it was entitled *The Red Confession* and the author was none other than himself. *I'm liking Crafter more and more. A man of exquisite tastes!*

Back to work...but what exactly *was* that? Well, he supposed he and the girls should go check the grounds for evidence of Crafter's grave, but a winding staircase to his right caught his eye and under it, an ornate nine-paneled door like those popular just before the Revolution. Centered on the door, however, was mounted what appeared to be a brass crucifix. The sunlight from the window struck the brass in an abstruse manner, causing it to radiate with an aura of whitish-green that seemed nearly molten. Something just as abstruse indicated that the Writer might be well advised to see what lay *behind* this door.

He turned the oval knob and, naturally, it was locked.

But this was not a hindrance, not now, was it? *My skills as an occult scientist make it such that no lock may bar my passage,* he thought jokingly. He went for the side table to retrieve the Hand of Glory, and—

It was gone.

And come to think of it, Snowie and Dawn still seemed to be gone as well.

Interesting.

The Writer was alone in the haunted house.

Fuck, he thought.

Did they take the Hand of Glory? And where did they go?

He tracked through inch-deep dust back to the door, then went onto the porch. "Snowie? Dawn?" No answer. *Maybe they're utilizing some initiative and started looking for Crafter's grave without having to be told*—he paused for a re-consideration—*or maybe not.* The Writer knew too well it was more likely they were off either smoking marijuana or performing mutual cunnilingus. Still, he didn't like the idea of their wandering around here—a cursed tract of land—by themselves.

He meandered across the front yard, half looking around and half keeping an eye out for the girls. The high grass of the property was several feel high but brown in death, and he wended between several ancient and appropriately ominous oak trees, at least one of which had no doubt been used to hang witches and condemned criminals. He wondered if *his* Hand of Glory had been derived from one such unfortunate, and decided the prospect offered a high order of probability.

At the edge of the woods that ringed the estate, he noticed a wrought-iron fence, waist high, half disintegrated by rust. This rested deeper in the woods and part of it had fallen or corroded completely, which did away with it as a fence with any practical function. *Inconsequential,* the Writer regarded. A far more nourishing food for thought was this: Mounted several feet before the rusted vestiges of the fence were planted (exactly seven feet apart—if he'd bothered to measure—seven, of course, being one of the *perfect* numbers) less-than conspicuous wooden posts, and on the front of each, the side facing the house, was a crucifix of what appeared to be very pitted and tarnished silver.

The perimeter, it seemed, is encircled by a fence of crosses, he thought. *Why would a SATANIST do such an illogical thing?* Crosses surrounding yards always faced out, so as to keep foul spirits from entering. *But these crosses face inward.*

The implication was clear. The *totemology* of this fence was meant to keep something on the *inside* from getting *out.*

The Writer found this observation enthralling but determined not to allow the conjecture to occupy his mind for long. *Big deal. If Crafter really was a magus genuinely empowered by the black arts, then that's one thing. But chances are he was probably just a crazy old kook...*

He got back to business: locating the girls and locating Crafter's grave. He'd have to stumble upon one or the other soon...and this he accomplished in quite a literal sense when he tripped in some sort of gully and fell over. *Shit! I'm too old to fall! I could break my hips!* He righted himself, groaning more than a little, and noticed with some surprise that he was very much standing within the confines of a graveyard, but not exactly a conventional one. No erected tombstones were in place, nor were there any traditional markers inlaid as we often find today, to increase the efficiency of the grass-cutting crews.

But there were markers in a sense, but these could only be called *ancient* markers, or more definitively *tabby* markers. Tabby was a crude and very inexpensive form of cement. In colonial times, the poorest of the poor would prepare this material, and dig a small hole before the grave of an interred person, and into that hole the tabby was poured and allowed to settle, and when it was just beginning to set, the bereaved—with his or her finger—would write the decedent's name and relative dates, and sometimes inscriptions as well. Tabby mortar, as it was named, proved useful in *unconsecrated* grounds too, where the corpse of a criminal or heretic would be buried. Even some of these lowly unfortunates had loved ones, and it was to the graveyard at night that such mourners trekked, with their tabby, to memorialize the dead.

The gully in which the Writer tripped possessed such a marker, which read in a barely legible scrawl: PURITY BOWEN, IN THE 17th YEAR OF HER LIFE, BY ASSIZE. 1697. *Ah,* the Writer thought, not having to be informed further. The word *assize* meant Miss Bowen, in the vigor of youth had been judicially done away with after having been found guilty of witchcraft, idolatry, or some other similar crime against God. And the gully was curious indeed: a five-foot-or-so long depression in the ground, oblong in configuration, and perhaps a foot and a half wide. *Somebody dug her body up a while ago—either in a coffin or in burlap,* the Writer figured. The bones of witches as well as the coffins of witches were valuable and much needed ingredients for the practiced "sorcerer."

It was no stretch to guess that Crafter himself, or some corrupted hireling, had disinterred the remains of the archaic Miss Bowen for use in his diabolisms.

Several more similar depressions could be noticed with a close eye many yards off; this unconsecrated tract seemed rather spacious for land originally belonging to a *British* colony. Here was one fractured marker which left enough to interpret: OLD MOTHER WILKINS, RONGLEY AKKUSED, 1608. *Wow, there's an old one,* thought the Writer, but the convict's absence from her grave suggested that she was probably *rytely* accused. With his pain-in-the-ass phone, he took a picture of the depressed plot. It might be just worthwhile to search the grounds with more diligence, to see what other enlivening inscriptions might be found.

But not *this* moment. For now, he felt he must find the girls.

His hunt did not take him much farther afield, his attention flagged by guttural moans and expletives which rang with a frowning familiarity. "Ugh! Fuck! I'm gonna, I'm gonna *come!*"

"Good! Do it! Do it on camera! Come your face off! Paulie'll love it!" said the other voice.

Of course, the vocal escapades belonged to Snowie and Dawn.

Shading his eyes up the yard, the Writer saw Dawn—but strangely not Snowie—lying stretched out on her stomach, wielding her camera phone.

Here is what he discovered: Dawn was indeed in a prone position, filming something, and what the something was, was Snowie, with her pants off, lying in another of the oblong depressions that had formerly served as a convict's grave. She was masturbating loudly and quite intensely, her hips and legs churning amid moans bordering on shrieks of irrepressible sexual pleasure, all of which merged at once into a convulsive, back-arching, hip bucking, eyeball-rolling climax.

The Writer frowned, covering his ears, for the sound was quite annoying. *Damn. Is that how girls have orgasms?* It was quite a show.

"Don't you girls have better things to do than lie in dug-up graves and masturbate?" he criticized. "I'm paying for your time, remember?"

"Damn, Snowie," Dawn said, kneeling up. "I've never seen you get off like that!"

Snowie lay immobile in the depression, staring upward in sheer bewilderment. "Good gosh'n holy everlivin' HAIL! That there was the best nut'a my whole life!"

"It must be that thing," Dawn speculated. "*Has* to be."

"Yeah, it must got *powers...*"

Par for the course, the Writer had no idea what they were talking about; instead he remained uselessly infuriated by the fact that either of his cohorts were even aware of his presence. But before he could yell at them, he made this observation:

Snowie was holding the Hand of Glory...

"You've got to be shitting me!" he bellowed. "You masturbated with *that* instead of your own hand? It's not a toy, Snowie, it's a very potent cabalistic device!"

Snowie chuckled in the grave. "I don't give a *shit* if it's somebody's cut-off hand. It made me come better'n I ever have—fuck!" Then she finally sat up in the depression, grinned at him. "Why'n'choo beat off with it? Bet it'll be the best nut'a yer life!"

"We're not here for *nuts,* Snowie!" he snapped (yet he had to admit the sight of her just then—bare-assed, bare-hipped, and spread-legged, with the shining white clump of pubic hair—did give him a momentary stir, in which he imagined himself lying atop of her in the grave, copulating away like Nero as Rome burned. But never mind that.) "Get out of there right now! And, Dawn, you ought to be ashamed of yourself for filming such a thing!"

"Are you kidding? A vid clip of a hot chick rubbing herself off with a *severed hand?* Paulie'll pay a hundred at least. Snowie? Give me the hand, now it's your turn to film me—"

"Bullshit!" the Writer shouted, pink in the face, and he snapped the hand from Snowie. "There'll be no more masturbating with severed hands! Now come on!"

The Writer marched back to the house, holding the withered Hand of Glory, while Snowie, who'd hauled her tight blue jeans back on, and Dawn, chuckled behind him.

But both girls howled when they entered the house behind him. "Holy *fuck!*"

"It's hotter than Afghanistan in here!" Dawn complained.

"And look at all this dust!" remarked Snowie of the accumulation on what appeared to be an Iranian eighteenth century throw rug, which she promptly expectorated on to clear dust from her throat. "Yuck!"

My God, thought the Writer. *What princess academy did she go to?...*

"And what a bunch of silly-ass furniture," Dawn said, looking around.

"Dawn, these are museum pieces!"

"Shit, you'd think a rich guy like Crafter would buy good stuff, like IKEA." And then she sat up on a ball-footed cherrywood table by famed Parisian cabinet-maker Alfred Emmanuel Beurdeley in 1870, inlaid with gold muses, approximate worth: $300,000.

"Oh, look!" Snowie delighted. "A Cadbury Easter egg! I love these things!"

"Me, too," Dawn said. "Give me half."

"I will, but I gotta open it. It's in some kind of a fancy holder…"

The Writer was near apoplectic. "Snowie! That's not candy, it's an iconic Imperial Egg by the House of Faberge! Only forty-three still exist!"

"Huh?" Snowie whined, digging at the object's jeweled, solid-gold girding. "Aw, fuck this, it won't open." And —*CLUNK*—she dropped it to the floor.

"What are we doing in here again?" Dawn chimed in with her own whine. "It's hot as fuck here—"

"Yeah!" Snowie agreed.

"You said you wanted to find Crafter's grave—"

"Okay," said the Writer. "You two go out and find it—"

"It's too hot!" the girls.

Female logic, he suspected. But one thing he couldn't object to was this: they both took off their tops in order to alleviate some of the stifling heat.

"Since it's so hot, I think a nice cold beer would do us all some good. Dawn, might you be good enough to see to that?"

She hopped off the Beurdeley table and proceeded to the cooler. Meanwhile, Snowie was using the Hand of Glory to scratch her back.

"Give me that!" he said and swiped it away. It actually hurt to tear his eyes off her sumptuous bare breasts, and then he got the double whammy when Dawn returned with the cooler, provocatively bending over to place it on the rosewood parquet flooring. The depending, chiffon-white breasts and gumdrop nipples swayed like a hypnotist's pendulum. *Great Gosh almighty, I've GOT to get my mind off these bimbos!*

She pulled a beer out for him, prepared to open it with her teeth, but the Writer howled: "No! Not like that! Find another way!" so she shrugged, looked around and, with a very skillful eye—*THUNK*—rammed the edge of the cap against an original Chippendale tulipwood Pembroke table made in 1754. The cap flew off the bottle without spilling a drop, and also cracked the edge of the priceless table.

All the Writer bothered to say was, "Dawn? I thank you, Dawn, and Thomas Chippendale thanks you."

His first swig of the ice-cold lager emptied a third of the bottle. *Ah, that did me good.* Thus he resumed his initial task, that of the door under the staircase, the *locked* door, and to this door he then deputed himself, now with the Hand of Glory. He was about to light the fingertips and recite the occult adjuration but—

A sound...

What IS that? Scratching?

Indeed, a light but very distinct scratching sound, as of fingernails on a wall, but he couldn't precisely discern whence it came. There it was again, more agitated. *What IS that?* "Hey, Dawn, come here quick. Do you hear that?"

She posed herself quite provocatively (as she was still topless, and her tits were sticking out like there was no tomorrow). "Yeah, yeah, I do. Sounds like someone scratching something, doesn't it?"

"That's exactly what I thought," the Writer said. "And it's curious. I've read a number of cases on demonic possession, and it's widely reported by witnesses and exorcists that 'scratching sounds' were heard regularly from behind walls and inside bed mattresses. The conclusion arrived at was that the scratching was generated by nearby demonic agencies…"

The scratching persisted, until Dawn turned, then frowned. "There's your demonic agency." She pointed. "It's Snowie scratching her hairy pussy!"

The Writer looked, then slumped in place. Sure enough, there was a very oblivious Snowie standing in the front parlor with her hand down the front of her pants, scratching away. She glared back at them. "What? Yawl act like you never seen a gal scratch her pussy hair before."

"Put a mower to that jungle," Dawn said.

"I gots me a better idea. I'll put a fist ta your face."

"Do yourself a favor. Put it to your own face—it'd make you prettier."

The Writer swigged more beer. *Just when things look like they're getting more interesting, they get more ridiculous.*

Naturally, a fight erupted in grand style, and the Writer backed away from it. *Fuck those redneck twits. Let 'em beat the daylights out of each other.* A cacophony arose of thunks, crashes, and priceless furniture breaking. Snowie expertly kicked Dawn right between the legs with a sound like an NFL punter. Dawn flew backwards and crashed into an 1888 Vitrine-style display purchased from Southeby's for $398,000, shattering all the glass and toppling dozens of invaluable imported knickknacks housed therein. But Dawn didn't miss a beat; she jumped up, unaffected, lifted a heavy oak-framed painting off the wall (an exquisite and virtually unknown 1801 oil of one Comte Donatien Alphonse François, also known as the Marquis de Sade in a yard-by-yard brass-framed shadow box), and heaved it in one swift motion at her adversary. Mr. De Sade's likeness burst spectacularly over Snowie's head, and then the stout frame hooked her neck, and yanked her horse-shoe style hard and face-first onto the rosewood and mother of pearl marquetry floor.

Then, with her artificial foot, Dawn kicked Snowie hard as she could right between the legs.

Snowie snapped into a fetal position, howling.

The Writer quickly lit the fingertips of the Hand of Glory, and began to recite the adjuration immediately in front of the mysterious door beneath the stairwell. Behind him more masterpieces of art and furniture cracked, split, and shattered; it was an infuriating distraction. He glanced aside a moment and saw Snowie sail across the room as if weightless, then heard an impressive thud, after which Dawn hopped after her, holding her artificial leg, tits bobbing.

The Writer finished the vocal rite, stepped back, and focused every dram of volition onto the door and to seeing it open.

One minute—nothing.

Two minutes—nothing.

Five minutes and it still hadn't opened. He grabbed the knob, turned, and pushed—

"MotherFUCKER!" he yelled. It was still locked.

At that moment, a plaster bust of Pallas flew by his face—missing him by an inch—and exploded to dust against the wall. "You fuckin' psychos!" he yelled at Snowie and Dawn amid more vicious thunks, thuds, and cracks. He tried the door again. Nothing, And then—

BOOM!

—the door in question imploded, cracking to pieces, because it had been impacted like a cannonball by the entwined bodies of Dawn and Snowie. The door broke down, and then the two topless girls disappeared down the basement steps into total darkness.

Ooo, thought the Writer. *That's not good. They got the damn door open but...are they still alive?*

He stepped into the black opening, feeling warm musty air gust up into his face. His pen light did nothing to provide illumination. "Snowie? Dawn? You girls okay?"

No answer came forth.

His tiny penlight also did nothing to penetrate the musty pitch-blackness of what descended. He knew his cell phone had a light in it but he felt he'd need an electrical engineering degree to find it. But at just that moment, he glanced aside and just inside the doorway saw something like a thermostat box, and on it was a button that read GENERATOR. *There's no way this generator will start after all these years,* but he pushed the button anyway. First, nothing, then a clank, and then...

The lights came on, and a swoosh of air-conditioning invaded the house. *Now, THAT'S fuckin' outstanding!* he thought. *The Great Goddess Lakshimi must be with me today!* He retrieved his beer, finished it, and plodded down the narrow steps, at the bottom of which remained Dawn entangled with Snowie. Snowie had Dawn in a headlock from behind, while Dawn was trying to hit Snowie in the head with her prosthesis. "You girls really do have problems," he said, stepping over them at the bottom. "You're gonna wind up killing each other, and then I'll *really* be pissed, because if you kill each other, then I'll have to dig up Crafter by myself, and I'm *too old* to do that!"

The Writer was about to pry them apart, but one glance into the basement stalled the impulse.

Six transoms were arranged around the stone-block room; they were doorways, and the doors themselves appeared to be fashioned from very old wooden planks nailed together, most likely oak or ash. The keystone of each transom was a large semi-precious gem, like amethyst, jasper, onyx, etc. More interesting—and more macabre—was the fact that high in the center of each door was an iron spike, and streaking down from each spike were copious brown stains: old blood. Yet something had already sparked in his memory: he'd seen these doors before, just as he'd seen the entire house before, a long time ago.

"These doors are interstices," he said aloud to himself.

Then his attention diverged momentarily, to another matter. *This girls...Are they dead? Did they kill each other?*

A swerve of his vision told him no...Well, *very much* no, actually, because at that moment, Dawn stood triumphantly over the still prostrate Snowie, standing on one leg, by the way, stump wagging, and she'd tactically positioned herself over Snowie's spread legs (and

Snowie, somehow, no doubt by some manner of "aid" from Dawn, had become divorced of her blue jeans and panties, if she'd been wearing any of the latter in the first place, from which her splayed crotch brazenly displayed a gorgeous clump of bright, white-blond hair bifurcated by a beautiful luminous-pink slit). Here, Dawn declared, "I'm gonna shove this leg up your silly albino bunny-rabbit cunt, and churn you like fuckin' butter!"

But, alas—poor Snowie was unconscious. The Writer snatched Dawn's leg from her hand. "What the fuck is wrong with you? Stop fighting right this instant if you want this leg back! Any more of this shit and I put the leg in there," and he pointed aside to something that looked like the hatch of a front-loading washer machine. The Writer already knew what it was...

"What's that?" Dawn snapped.

"It's a propane crematory, much older than the one at your funeral parlor. It kicks up to over 2,000 degrees, which will melt this leg like a Clark bar. You'll have to *hop* all the way to VA to get a new one."

Dawn looked bewildered at the odd hatch and its rusty brand-name plaque: Ener-Tek IV. "You wouldn't dare! I'm a handicapped combat veteran!"

No more Mr. Nice Guy. The Writer opened the hatch, threw the artificial leg in, and locked it shut. Then his finger raised to the IGNITE button.

"Okay! Okay!" Dawn conceded.

"I thought so." The Writer took the leg out of the machine. "Now help Snowie up."

"Fuck, no! I'm not helping that redneck bitch!"

"I'll punch you in the face," the Writer said with no hesitation.

Dawn laughed. "No you won't! Only a scumbag would punch a female amputee standing on one leg—"

WHAP!

Yes, the Writer's meager fist socked Dawn right in the eye, with formidable impact, and down she went. When her bare back slapped the stone floor, her breasts jiggled in a manner that could only be described as sensational.

Twenty minutes later, the Writer had both girls up and conscious, and forced them to make up, which was easier than he'd suspected. *Violence begets lust,* he guessed. Dawn had her leg back on and was squashing Snowie against a wall and lip-locking her while Snowie, still totally nude, seemed close to the throes of orgasm. Both girls had black eyes, which provided an interesting contrast.

"Any day now, girls. Come on, we have work to do."

Tits pressing, the women looked around, half-oblivious. "Wow, what is this freaky place?" Dawn asked.

"This is Crafter's basement?" Snowie asked. "It's the most up'n fucked up basement I ever seen."

"This is a *nave,* Snowie, or a *chancel…*that is, a satanic one," elucidated the Writer. "A temple to the devil. It was here that Crafter practiced his occult sciences, among which was an art called Tephramancy, an ancient chemistry which utilizes the ashes of a sacrifice victim for a variety of dark arts, including incarnation."

But Snowie's attention had already lapsed, as she strode nude to the first gem-transomed door. She opened it—

"The fuck kind'a door is this?" came her mystified exclamation. "It don't lead to nowhere."

Dawn frowned at the solid bricks behind the old wood-plank door. "But since Crafter was a warlock, maybe these doors are really—"

"They're called *traversion bridles,*" said the Writer. "And if you believe in the supernatural, they most likely *are* doorways."

"Doorways to where?"

"Well, for one thing, to Hell. And God only knows where else. Ethereal planes, other dimensions, even other worlds if the papyri of Hermes Trismegistus can be regard as accurate." He stared fixedly at one of the doors.

Finally, the expected question was asked, by Dawn. "How are they opened?"

"Fuck you, Dawn!" Snowie blurted. "We *ain't* openin' 'em! I don't wanna go to Hell!"

"Shit, Snowie. We live in West Virginia; we're already *in* Hell."

You haven't seen Jersey, the Writer thought. "All jokes aside, according to many a magus, these bridles can indeed be opened with the proper invocations, sacrifices, and sundry other supplications."

Snowie's bare breasts jiggled awesomely when she blurted, "Fuck all'a this! This place is fucked up—let's go back to town. I wanna go to the bar and drink!"

The Writer's brow popped up. As much as he'd like to take Snowie's advice, there was still much work to be done. However, a cold Collier's Lager would work quite nicely now. "Since I'm old and fat, would one of you girls be good enough to go upstairs and bring down some beers?"

"I ain't goin' up there by myself," Snowie asserted. "This place is haunted!"

"Reportedly by ghosts *and* demons," the Writer added with a smile.

"Shit," Dawn scoffed. "If I see any ghosts or demons, I'll beat the shit out of 'em."

"Good girl."

Dawn disappeared up the enclosed stairwell with a surprising agility for someone with one leg, but—

With even more agility, she sped back down.

"What? Where's the beer?" asked the Writer.

Dawn's acumen and attitude instantly demanded whispers. "There's someone upstairs!"

All three froze where they stood, and the Writer, ordinarily bright, mentally reactive, and capable of quick decision-making, was suddenly locked in cerebral vapor-lock.

Next: sturdy, deliberate footsteps descended the stairs.

Police, guessed the Writer, in which case he could probably bribe them now that he was a millionaire. But...

What if it's a ghost or demon? What if it's...the Bighead?

Before any more suppositions could transpire in the Writer's head, the interloper stepped onto the landing and was revealed at last, not a monster or supernatural manifestation, and not a policeman.

It was, instead, a black man with a gun.

***

"Hooooooooooly *shit!*" Tucker Larkins yelled when he, ahead of his brothers Gut and Clyde, walked into the side door of the barn and easily noticed the naked, perfectly still, and very skinny brunette lying on her back on the dirt floor.

"A splittail!" celebrated Gut. "Look like a creeker gal!"

Tucker nodded, unconsciously giving himself a crotch-squeeze as he always did whenever he had the opportunity to eyeball a helpless naked woman. "Bet she's one of Mr. Nayle's what like he keeps in his chicken pens fer a while when he catch 'em stealin' corn."

Clyde was chuckling, impressed. "More likely'n not this is Horace's work. That boy shore think up some nifty ways ta lay down a ruckin' on a gal. But...dang! Look at her face..."

Indeed, her face—if it could be called that—was so swollen by some manner of infection that it more resembled a deep-dish pizza or a strawberry pie with all the crust peeled off.

"She dead?" Gut inquired. "Shore look it."

Clyde approached the still woman and knelt.

"You gonna check her pulse?" Tucker asked.

Clyde smirked. He wasn't picky, though in truth none of the boys were strangers to engaging in intercourse with women who were no longer among the living, and Clyde was "laying pipe" in not much more time than it took to pull his jeans down.

Tucker said to Gut, "Come on. Let's get us a cold beer and find Horace. I needs ta know what he done ta that gal's face. That boy's a dang genius! Like them Einstein fellas who invent the atom bomb and those bagel shops!"

They left Clyde to his urgent business, and made loping redneck tracks to the stream that provided their auxiliary beer cooler.

Tucker stopped in his tracks and yelled, "Hoooooly—"

"FUCK!" Gut finished.

Of course, as the reader has already been made aware, there wasn't much left of Horace waiting for them, just great flaps of fat as if he'd swallowed a stick of dynamite. A variety of other internal organs were strewn all about in quite a radius. Great loops of intestines festooned nearby trees to present a unique and colorful image, though Gut and

Tucker were of an ilk not likely to appreciate such a manifestation.

Gut began blubbering at once. "Someone up'n done the job on our dear brother! Someone blowed him up!"

Tucker, though the same age as Gut, was possessed of a higher level of maturity, and instead of exhibiting emotional breakdown, he remained more reserved, contemplative, and reactive. "That they did, Gut, that they did, and we'se gonna find out who it was'n do him worse. Bet it were one'a these 'spanick fellas always comin' in here trine ta sell thur heroin. We cain't kill them buggers fast enough, and now's they want revenge."

"Yeah," Gut blubbered a distracted agreement.

"But whose-ever they was, they done more'n blow our brother up." Tucker pointed down to the fleshy shell of the corpse. "They tore off his junk as well."

They had, all right, for in the area of space that should have been occupied by Horace's penis and testicles there was just a meaty wound, with the clear suggestion that the genitals had been *ripped*— not cut—off the body.

Gut sniffled, perplexed, with hitches in his voice. "That's-that's-that's plum crazy! What-what they do with his package, Tuck? They run off with it?"

Tucked grimly shook his head; he was by far more observant than Gut. "Them devils didn't take it no farther than that there tree," and he pointed again.

Hanging limply from the indicated tree was something like... well, no simile comes to mind accurate enough to put the reader in possession of the image the two brothers then beheld.

Horace's scrotum had been hooked onto a short tree branch, where it, the testicles, and the understandably flaccid penis all hung heavily, swaying like a modern-art pendulum. It would've made a great painting by Dali.

Tucker turned in an authoritative pose. "Now Gut, just you go git Clyde'n tell what up'n happened, and you two head out east a bit. You boys do ever-thang ya can ta catch the fuckers done this to poor Horace. Me, I'll be headin' west a bit, doin' the same. We'll meet back here at eight tonight. Got it?"

Gut faltered, nodding reluctantly. "Yuh-yeah, Tuck, but..aw, hell. Muh-muh-maybe it wasn't none'a them 'spanick fellas after all. Muh-muh-maybe..."

Tucker, more patient then most, was getting testy. "Maybe *what?*"

A dreadful thought propped open Gut's eyes. "Maybe it were... the Bighead."

Tucker shook his head, annoyed. "Talk some sense, Gut. Ain't no such thing as the Bighead. That's just one'a them, what they call, *fables.*"

"Buh-buh-but Carrie Kline say she heard from Richie Eads wife that she heard from Boyd Waller that he heard from Millie Slat that she seed the Bighead stompin' through the woods this very mornin', buck nek-it and stinkin' ta high heaven. Twelve foot tall, she say, and a pecker flappin', like, almost a *yard long.*"

Tucker pinched the bridge of his nose. "Gut, Gut—Millie Slat's *retarded.* She got the *brain* damage ever since she got hit'n in the head accidental by that nail gun. Jigged up her brain somethin' fierce, it did. Thinks her name's Molly'n thinks she live in Kentucky. Hail, she *still* call the state police ever Christmas Eve sayin' Santa Claus is comin' down her chimney trine to lay some peckerwood on her and—shee-it! She ain't even *got* a chimney!"

"Buh-buh-but—yuh-you said yer own self years ago that Bighead were real, said you up'n *saw* him back near Jake Martin's old shack near Tick Neck Road..."

"Well, you're right, Gut, I did say that, but that weren't nothin', see? I 'member that, and I were inside Martin's shack trine ta git me a piece'a pussy off'a Barb Croter but she's all pitchin' a fit whinin' 'bout how she gotta *save* herself fer the man she up'n marry. Well, fuck—if that ain't the dumbest thing I ever heerd! Anyway, I 'ventually make a deal with her. She say she'll suck my dick'n swaller the nut, but onlys if I eat her pussy first. Well, hail, I'se a natural man'n I like ettin' a gal's snatch just like the next guy, so's she push off them trampy shorts'a hers, set her big ass right up on the edge'a that big table in there'n I put my face right 'tween them fat gams, and—hot dobbin'n holy *hail!* That gal's pussy smelt *so bad,* that I got dizzy and 'twas gaggin' and my eyes waterin'. Just *one sniff,* I tell ya, it was like I got hit in the face with a fuckin' *cinderblock,* it was! Now, don't git me wrong; I've *smelt* me some bad pussy in my day, and I mean *really* bad pussy, and I've always kind'a liked it. But *this?* Ho-boy! Like a dead possum on the road for three days in summer—well, no, shee-it—a *hunnert* times worse than that. I've smelt *creeker* pussies not half this bad, and you know them 'ho's—they don't warsh but once a month or so. Dang, Gut, 'twas like Barb Croter ain't never warshed her pussy in her *whole fuckin' life,* it was! No lie, right then'n there I bend over and throwed up. And you know what that sassy bitch say? She say 'What's the matter, sugar? Afraid of a little musk?' Musk, huh? Shee-it. Anyways, that stink fucked me up for *days.* T'was enough ta mess with any fella's senses. And that's when, as I was runnin' out'a that there shack, I thunk I seed the Bighead. But I'se shore it weren't *really* the Bighead I seen, t'was just a *pussy-stank 'lucination,* it was." Tucker stalled momentarily, and seemed a bit wobbly on his feet, brought a hand to his considerable belly, and said, "Shuh-shee-it, all this talk 'bout Barb Croter's pussy make me think I just might throw up again," and then he paled, hitched in place, and emptied all the day's viddles out his mouth in a single mammoth, splattering plume.

So much for the disquisition on feminine odors.

"Just go do as I tolt ya—" Tucker barked, and began to ineffectually jog west, in pursuit of the true villain who'd killed so horribly his wonderful brother Horace.

Just as ineffectually, Gut jogged back to the barn to educate Clyde as to what had happened, all the while reflecting, *Dang! That must'a been some really BAD pussy stink,* and now that he thought of it, to this day, Barb Croter remained unmarried.

Gut had a pretty good idea why.

***

"Case," the black man answered when the Writer inquired of his name. "Just call me Case. My real name doesn't matter; I believe I was named at an orphanage, but who cares? The only name that really matters is the name God gives us when He writes our names in the Book of Life."

The Writer's mouth fell open, and he thought *Holy Roller,* but then this black-dressed black man—Case—didn't fit the rest of the bill, especially the pistol in his hand, but this he'd banished to his jacket pocket when he'd discerned that no danger awaited him from a fat, out of shape sixty-year-old man, a topless woman with one leg, and another woman—an *albino*—fully naked and with a black eye.

The Writer had to smile. *What a scenario to walk into...* "Dawn, Snowie, the show's over, now's a good time to put your clothes back on."

Both women disappeared up the stairs, giggling and, of course, with their breasts bouncing spectacularly.

The expected followed. "Case" briefly explained himself, as if in a minor annoyance. Though his black shoes, slacks, shirt, and jacket made him appear to exist in some official clerical employment, it was actually "unofficial." He described himself instead as "something of a custodian for a branch for the Catholic Diocese of Richmond," which sounded to the Writer quite a convoluted statement. It sounded like subterfuge or camouflage for something else. Case was not a priest, did not expect in the fullness of time to pursue priest's orders, was not a seminarian nor a deacon, but lived to "serve God and only God," which he said with no trace of pomp whatsoever. It was as though he were talking about baseball, or what he had for lunch.

"It's none of my business," the black man said next, "but...those two girls? They're not your daughters, are they?"

The notion amused the Writer very much. "Hardly. They're just friends; you might say they're *my* custodians, I pay them for various errands that I'm too old or lazy to do myself, and to drive me around. But speaking of driving...did you park at the end of the drive behind the white El Camino? You drove here, right?"

"I parked my church car on the other side of the hill, hiked up through the woods, and hopped the fence."

"So I presume you know about this house, otherwise why else would you be here?" the Writer went on.

"Oh, yes. The house of a warlock."

"And you *believe* that?"

Case nodded. "Yes. Just as *you* do." He smiled. "Otherwise, why else would *you* be here?"

This was getting weirder by the minute.

"Well, we're both trespassers, we're both here without any authorization, therefore, we owe each other no explanations as to why we're here," the Writer said. "But do you mind if I ask?"

"Why am I here?" Case said. "Let's just say an impulse brought me here."

"An *impulse?*"

"That's right. I have uncannily accurate impulses, I might say."

"So you were just driving down the road for no reason in particular and an *impulse* occurred to you to pull immediately over and come up here?"

The sarcasm seemed to amuse the black man. "You're right, I'm not being very up front, am I? The church dispatched me to a property—that is, a *church* property—not far from here. It's called Wroxton Abbey."

An abbey... The Writer's eyes opened wide. *Didn't the girls mention something about an ABBEY around here? Yes! They told me last night it's where the Bighead died!*

"Well, I lost my way, and the map the church gave me is very dated," the black man continued. "And since I was in the area, I thought I'd stop by here. There's quite a file on this place—and its previous owner—at the Diocese."

The answer seemed reasonable. Then the Writer offered, "My two associates—once they get their clothes back on—might know the location of this abbey you're in search of."

"That would be great!"

"And if you're wondering why *we* are here, it's because, well—"

"We're here to dig up a corpse!" Snowie blurted as both girls blundered back down the steps, both fully dressed, and both exhibiting an extreme case of the giggles.

Case, with a raised brow, looked at the Writer.

"It's a long story," was all the Writer could say. "You'll just have to trust me on that."

"Fair enough," said Case.

"Don't feel bad," Dawn said. "He won't tell us either, and that really sucks for me 'cos *I'm* the one who's gotta dig up the grave."

"Looking for ciphers, would be my guess," Case said, more to himself.

Now the Writer's brow rose. *Ciphers?* "Why do you say that?"

"Well, for thousands of years, warlocks, sorcerers, magi, etc., have all engaged in the practice of going to their graves with their most significant secret. Crafter certainly knew this, so why wouldn't he practice it himself? From what I understand, he had quite the ego, and he was very *into* being a warlock."

Ciphers... Why else would my doppelganger tell me to dig up the guy's dead body? The Writer shrugged. *I guess the best way to find out is...*

"Do you know what this room is?" Case asked.

"A sacrificial chancel," the Writer replied. "And these six doors are what the good Dr. John Dee referred to as Talismanic Traversion Bridles."

Case seemed impressed. "How did you come to know *that?* It's very, very obscure information. Most historians and archaeologists wouldn't know the purpose of this place."

"I went to Harvard *and* Yale," the Writer attempted a joke. "I learned *all kinds* of obscure and mostly useless things."

Case pinched his chin. "Harvard and Yale. But you're a *novelist?*"

How the hell does he know that? wondered the Writer. "Oh, you must've read one of my books and recognized me from the author photo." And before Case could say "No," the Writer went forth with his stock in trade explanation of his professional ideology: "I'm a writer," he said. "I travel all over the country. I need to see different things, different people. I need to see life in its different temporal stratas. I come to remote towns like this because they're variegated. They exist separately from the rest of the country's societal mainstream. Towns like this are more *real*. So, yes, I'm a writer, I'm a novelist. But, in a more esoteric sense, I'm a *seeker*."

"A seeker," Case repeated. Was he trying not to frown?

"Well, that's an abstraction, of course," the Writer went on. "What I mean is I'm on a quest. I'm searching for some elusive uncommon denominator to perpetuate my aesthetic ideologies. For a work of fiction to exist within any infrastructure of resolute meaning, its peripheries must reflect certain elements of truth. I don't mean objective truths. I'm talking about ephemeral things: *unconscious* impulses, *psychological* propensities, etc.—the *underside* of what we think of as the human experience. Honesty is the vehicle of my aesthete. The truth of fiction can only exist in its bare words. Pardon my obtuseness, but it's the *mode,* the *application* of the vision which must transcend the overall tangibilities. Prose mechanics, I mean—the structural manipulation of syntactical nomenclatures in order to affect particularized transpositions of imagery. So, *that's* why I'm a novelist."

The Writer felt certain that Case would be impressed with this sophisticated verbal thesis.

Case did not seem impressed. "So, your being a novelist is the reason you're standing in a warlock's basement?"

The Writer thought about that. "I...guess you're right."

"Let me continue, if I may. You're familiar with some specifics of occult science. You know the function of this room and the things in it. And you know that Ephriam Crafter very much *believed* in those occult sciences. He believed that the things in this room *work.* He *sacrificed* women in this room. He *impaled them* on the spikes sticking out of these doors. And after he had issued the proper supplications, he *believed* that these doors would open as passageways to the netherworld." Case looked directly into the Writer's eyes. "Do *you* believe that?"

The Writer felt momentarily tongue-tied. He stared, unblinking, until his eyeballs felt dry. Then an image popped hard into brain: the extra-large embalming table at Dawn's funeral parlor: empty.

"Yes. I believe that," the Writer said, "and at this point...I don't *dis*believe anything."

"That's great to hear." Case seemed relieved by the assertion; he pulled up a folding chair, sat down, and said, "Now. Tell me about this gig of yours. Digging up Crafter's body."

***

You've seen the type of bus to which I allude: like school buses only much shorter—the word "squab" comes to mind, not as of an unfledged pigeon but the old Victorian adjective meaning short and fat. I suppose the bus I have in mind is a Type 2 International Harvester, popular in the '80s—*a specialty bus,* in that it was much shorter than what most are driven to school in. Those seated seventy to eighty riders, but this bus only accommodated twelve. In other words, looking at it head on, you would think it was a standard school bus, but a side view showed you how severely short it was. And whereas the good old-fashioned school buses we're used to are yellow, with black letters, *this* school bus had been painted a dreary "institutional" gray; nor were there any side windows, and by now you may have guessed why.. I'm confident that you've all seen these vehicles on the road at one time or another: indeed, nothing less than a prison transport bus.

The particular bus to which I beg your attention was now traveling a winding forest-lined state road—no matter which—and was currently engaged in the task of taking three inmates to the nearest hospital for routine medical checkups. You would know what manner of persons were our inmates by merely reading the side of the drab little bus: BOONE COUNTY WOMEN'S DETENTION CENTER.

In this cold-hearted day and age, many typical taxpayers would argue the legitimacy of providing *anything* other than emergency medical care to the piles of human flotsam—mostly drug addicts, mind you, guilty and convicted of drug-related crimes and other illicit acts that so threatened the status quo—that clogged our penal system and sucked the nation's coffer dry. But *this* case might be deemed an exception by even the most strident naysayers of human compassion.

Our three female wards of the system, see, were all late in their third trimesters of pregnancy, so the Powers That Be thought it necessary to afford these convicts effective prenatal care, to insure that the forthcoming trio of little bundles of joy alight onto the earth as healthily as possible.

This seemed a reasonable expense, even to Republicans.

Now it's time to introduce you to the occupants of our little gray bus; we'll start with our three lady passengers (mind you, the term "lady" may well be too charitable a designation).

First: Mitchell, Bertha, Caucasian, age 32. This woman *looked* like a Bertha; she stood 6'2" and weighed 250 when she *wasn't* pregnant. Her cellblock name was Bigfoot. She was always quite ready to settle her differences with her fists, which she did with some efficacy, and it was not likely that "good behavior" might one day lead to early release for the "dime" she'd been sentenced to for killing her grandmother for insurance money.

Second: Green, Kimberly, Caucasian, age 30. 5'6", pretty in a white trash kind of way...maybe, and tipping the scale at about 130 without child, and twenty of that was tits—hence the nickname: "Tits." Her mouth was as dirty as it was deft, at least according to a good many detention officers, male and female alike.

Third: Broomfield, Monica, Caucasian, age 28. She weighed 120 *with* the thirty pounds of baby, placenta, and amniotic fluid stuffed in her stomach. She hadn't the loud, boisterous, shit-talking mouths that the other two had but, also, like the other two, any occasion that presented itself for that mouth to be filled with cock...well, Ms. Broomfield was amenable to that. You see, in prison, favors were bestowed more readily to inmates willing to make use of their mouths, if you receive my meaning. Her nickname was "Bo Peep," because it suited her very passive demeanor. She would do her five-year stint scarcely uttering a word or leaving a footprint.

Readers of a more visual bent will wonder why no mention has been made of our ladies' hair-colors, styles, or lengths. Well, that's because a head-lice outbreak made it necessary for the authorities to "cue-ball" every woman in the prison, and each and every hairy armpit and pubic patch had been buzzed to non-existence. It will be added, for the sake of thoroughness, that Bertha's aka Bigfoot's pubic area had been especially abundant, and at the finish of her "de-hairing," it looked like a moderately sized woodchuck had fallen asleep between her feet.

Your narrator forgot to mention a possibly pertinent detail, in that the three women all sat on the right side of the bus, affording the driver better visual surveillance from the inside rearview, and each of their right hands were cuffed at the wrist and chained to the seat. They also wore attractive ankle-bracelets, the true sign of a woman with class!

Mind you, it is my every effort to communicate these "incidental" details in an economic fashion, but I deem it relevant to add some "color" to the question of what our inmates were dressed in. Typically, all of the incarcerated at the Boone's County facility wore fluorescent-orange jumpsuits with bold black letters on front and back reading PRISONER. Uniformity was important for it helped keep the women "cowed" by stripping them of aspects of individuality, and then there was the idea that the vivid color would make them all the more visible in the event of elopement (that's what they called escape these days—elopement).

Ah, but our pregnant friends here were so far along in their terms by now that the jumpsuits didn't fit, so they were given an alternative; gowns, of sorts, of the same loud orange color, more like ponchos without hoods. These garments had snaps in front at various distances, such that each gown could be adjusted for a more proper fit, but overall, the visual effect made each woman look like a walking orange pup tent with a shaved head sticking out on top, and a basketball-sized stomach sticking out in front. All prisoners, too, wore orange flip-flops.

There. The descriptions of the inmates are now complete. And as much as the author of these words would thrill to detail further information of the personal experiences of Bigfoot, Tits, and Bo Peep, it is by no means part of my plan to do so (even as entertaining as it would be) because the end of this story might never be reached.

Naturally, it goes without saying that our three transportees were not unaccompanied on their journey to the hospital in the stubby gray bus. Two "authority figures" were present as well, as we would all reasonably expect, and they were both "D.O.s," which stood for detention officer.

One: Sergeant Harding Ryans, who drove the bus. He was a prison employee in good stead—hence the reason that he was one of very few men working in this exclusively female prison (which many would consider a howling if not a flat-out Sears-Tower-sized administrative error due to the gentleman's actual deeds and character). Tall, slim, and dark-haired, he could pass for twenty but was probably forty, and when in the presence of his professional associates, he displayed an acumen of impressive courtesy, politeness, and bearing, a man of good breeding and quality education, as well as a man of compassion and consideration.

But all of these wonderful traits went straight out the window when in the presence of persons who were *not* his professional associates—namely, the inmates. For instance, there was not *one single incarcerated mouth* in the entire facility that had not been filled with the good sergeant's semen on numerous occasions, even the "grannies" and, yes, even the 600-pounder in D Wing. "Put your mouth up to the bars and suck my dick, or I'll mace you in the face," he'd told her upon his first meeting. While many related to the Shakespearian simile "All the world's a stage," Ryans' observation was "All the world is a tramp's mouth."

Unlike most of the male D.O.'s, Ryans did *not* partake in vaginal intercourse with any inhabitant of the penitentiary, for surely the vaginas of such a lot were *seething* with venereal organisms, and he did *not* wish to display walnut-sized genital sores to the prison doctor at his next physical. Alas, oral sex could get dull several times a day over years, so he reasoned, for variety's sake, that "butt-germs" were probably not nearly as virulent as "cooter-germs." In other words, Ryans was quite the Back Door Butler when on rounds, and many times had he uttered, poker-faced, "Put your bare ass against the bars and spread your cheeks, or I'll mace you in the face." This message was always received loud and clear, and it was into the rectums of many an inmate that he had enjoyed the privilege of giving a little of the old "peckersnot enema."

But hear me out.

These were not the *only* kind of "enemas" Ryans doled out. Without going into prurient detail—and counting on the astute reader to make use of simple deduction—I'll add only that in Sergeant Ryans' *years* as an employee of the prison, he had not once ever urinated in the guards' lavatory.

Ryans, by the way, was not married, never had been, and had no girlfriend. Why the FUCK would he need any of that in this concrete wonderland of orgasmic outlets?

Two: Captain Philip Straker, who was the transport captain. With him rested the responsibility of seeing to the safety of the inmates to and from their destinations, and of seeing that all such journeys went without mishap—no elopements, in other words, and never once had such a thing occurred on his watch. Medium height, fat, gray and balding, he was often mistaken for a man in his seventies rather than a man at the back end of his fifties, which was probably attributable to decades of smoking, drinking, and eating junk food, including hundreds of proverbial donuts.

He bragged quite often about all the "pussy" and "suck jobs" he got at the prison. "Over the years I been here, shit, I've fucked *thousands* of these criminal slut-bags. That's all they know, all the bitches exist for—to suck, swallow, and get fucked. Oh, and to get their asses kicked whenever they get mouthy. Best way to teach 'em the way things are in life, you teach 'em with your dick and then your billy. Yes sir, first, you fuck 'em, then you fuck 'em *up*. You're doin' 'em a favor actually, 'cos if you don't kick 'em in the cunt or clout 'em in the chops every now and then, they'll just go on breakin' the law for the rest of their junkie, hosebag lives. They need to learn: justice *hurts*. And never, *ever* beat the shit out of a girl without fuckin' her. It's a waste, a waste of pussy. Shit, any girl in this Cement Ramada got it comin', and it's every D.O.'s right to get his wang in as much convict gash as he can."

So saith big bad Captain Straker, but like most men at the end of the day, he was all talk, and in truth his "wang" hadn't been in any "convict gash" for twenty years. Why is this? one might ask. Why had he not discreetly taken advantage of utilizing all of the surplus joy-holes in the facility, as most had? The answer is easily within reach: you see, for the last twenty years, Straker had been taking Paul-Bunyan-sized doses of blood-pressure medicine. Mind you, this medicine worked very well, and it kept the blood pressure way down, but it also kept some other things way down as well.

So much for the requisite character sketches of the occupants of our stubby little bus. And now on with the adventure...

"Look at ya all's," Straker complained, standing shotgun. "Pieces of human shit, never any of ya worked a real job in your lives, all on the welfare and the food cards, fuck ten scumbags a day to get knocked up on purpose, got pussies on ya big enough to drive this bus through and bellies full'a God knows what. Ought to be ashamed'a yourselves, the lot of ya. Only things ya do right is eat and fuck, and stuff your faces with Twinkies and Pop Tarts the taxpayers buy and then push it out your dirty assholes. Then America's gotta pay for the flush."

Bo Peep curled up into a ball and started to sob. Tits was picking her nose, looking out the non-existent window, and Bigfoot scratched her crotch through the orange "gown." "We love you too, Captain," she said. "Thanks for the kind words—what a nice guy!"

"Am I gonna have trouble with you?" Straker said. He wore two Tasers on his belt like six guns, and pulled one out. "If so, I'll end that shit right now."

"Big man," the largest of the inmates mocked. "Likes to talk shit to defenseless pregnant women chained to a fuckin' bus. What a hero. Need to do shit like this to feel like a *real* man, huh? What a sissy, what a fat pathetic little homo. I know little girls tougher than you, ya old shit."

D.O. Straker stared. He glanced back at Ryans behind the wheel. "Sergeant Ryans, did you hear what this human garbage can just said to me?"

"I sure did, Captain. And if the convict knows what's good for her, she'll keep her cocksucker closed for the rest of this trip."

"Fuck you, too, ya skinny fuck-tard," Bigfoot yapped back.

"You can talk all the abusive shit ya want, but neither of you can do anything to us and you both know it."

"Is that so?" Straker smiled with hands on hips. "Ya hear that Ryans? We can't do anything to these dirty jizz-buckets."

Bigfoot blared, pointing. "Because there's a fuckin' *camera* right there! Everything you do and say is recorded!"

Straker and Ryans both paused, then erupted laughter. "Oh, that old aisle camera up there? We got it set on a—" Straker snapped his fingers. "What's it called, Sergeant?"

"A feed loop," said the driver with a smile. "It just records the first ten minutes of the trip, then loops it over and over. Easy to rig."

Bigfoot contemplated these words with narrowed eyes, then frowned wide. "That's bullshit. The tech people at the prison would know."

"Oh, so you don't believe me, huh? Well, okay, but tell me this. How could I punch you in the face if I was bullshitting?" Then—THWACK!— Straker rammed his fist as hard as he could into Bigfoot's left cheekbone.

"Mother*fucker!*" the woman bellowed, bringing her free hand to her face.

"Dang, Ryans. Looks like the inmate fell down and landed on her face when she was getting on the bus."

"I'll put it in my transport log, Captain. Gotta be thorough."

"And how's this for bullshit, Slim?" Straker yanked Bigfoot's orange maternity gown all the way up, exposing big pallid-white flops of breasts and the gargantuan beach-ball-sized belly. He began to feel up those breasts with gusto. "What's about this? Am I molesting you? Isn't this *sexual harassment* of a female prisoner? Won't the camera see me doing it?" There came more gruff laughter. "Gee, I'm gonna get fired, ain't I? Please don't sue me, Bigfoot!" THWACK!—went another fist to the face.

With her free hand—THWACK!—Bigfoot repaid the Captain's kindness with a punch right in the crotch. This punch, by the way, was much more forceful than either of Straker's had been, and evidently she'd hit the sweet-spot, because Straker collapsed at once to the floor, making cow-like moos of agony.

Tits howled behind her and managed a high-five. "About time that fuck got one in the nuts!" Bo Peep, however, did not share in the celebration; instead she remained curled up in her seat, knees as close to her face as her gravid belly would allow, sobbing. She clearly was not cut out for these sorts of entanglements. She may even have been sucking her thumb.

Meanwhile, during all the action, Sergeant Ryans calmly pulled the bus into a strip mall parking lot, parked, unseated himself, walked down the aisle, stepped over Straker who was still clutching his crotch and mooing, then maced Bigfoot in the face. The oversized woman howled banshee-like and covered her face in a reactive gesture that was utterly useless. Then, for good measure, Ryans pulled off her triple-extra large panties, winced at her morass of a bald vagina, and then maced that as well.

Now Bigfoot convulsed in her seat, sort of *jiggling*, kind of like a Mexican Jumping Bean (if you *remember* Mexican Jumping Beans) and the noises escaping her throat pretty much defied description (hence, I won't bother trying to reproduce them here).

In a few moments, Ryans got his superior seated and re-composed. "Take a breather, Captain. We're over an hour early so why don't I drive us out to the...you know, the special place? Good idea?"

The winded Captain Straker huffed and nodded.

And...what of this "special place?"

Many horror novels make use of, say, a clearing in the woods. These clearings are barely plausible but very convenient when an author needs a secluded setting in which antagonistic characters can take innocent woman and do...mean things to them, and to thereby revel in the lambasted genre tool known as gratuitousness. You likely know the manner of locale to which I refer.

That said, we now find our squat little gray bus and its occupants effectively settled in our clearing, where some aberrant activity was now taking effect. The vehicle is parked, the motor off, and Sergeant Ryans has just walked up to Bo Peep (with his penis out, mind you), and he has just said, "Okay, Bo Peep. You know the drill," as into the introverted little inmate's mouth his turgid business deputed itself.

Bigfoot was still shuddering in her seat, keening and howling in agony. While such ungainly noises most men might find too much of a distraction to have an orgasm, this was *not* the case with our Sergeant Ryans. The vociferations, actually, had an opposite effect on the detention officer, and in less time than it takes you to say "immediate," his spermatic cargo was transferred into the wan little Bo Peep's mouth. She did not need to be asked or told to swallow.

Ryans leaned back on the edge of the next seat. "You're the perfect woman. You never say a word and you swallow without complaining. If you weren't a fucked up useless white-ghetto piece of convict trailer trash, I might have to marry you."

Bo Peep considered these words and, par for the course, began to sob.

Eventually, Ryans redirected his attention to his superior, and when he saw what was about to happen, he yelled, "Captain! What the fuck are you doing?"

Straker was standing now, recovered enough from his painful assault, and he had drawn one of his Tasers and was pointing it at Bigfoot. "This bitch punched me in the balls! *No one* punches me in the balls and gets away with it!"

And as Heaven is my witness that I am telling only the bare truth, Captain Straker at this moment discharged his Taser at none other than Bigfoot's huge uncovered belly. The non-lethal weapon made an interesting PAP! sound when its trigger was squeezed; this was the sound of two barbed electrode darts being launched from the device via, not gunpowder but compressed nitrogen, and when those darts sunk into the inmate's swollen belly, there came an immediate and unmistakable crackling "electric" noise which was the sound of a five-second release of 50,000 volts into the "target."

Well, if Bigfoot thought that a couple swats to the face and getting maced in the vagina was bad, only now did she learn what *bad* really was. Her Mexican Jumping Bean imitation was insignificant compared to what followed: a five-second infusion of incomparable "soul-searing" agony marked by violent convulsions that had her football player-sized frame appearing almost to levitate. And of course she was screaming holy hell like someone, say, being slowly fed into an industrial plastic shredder.

"Yeah? Like that, honey?" Straker mocked to her. "Bet that feels good, huh?"

"For fuck sake, Captain!" Ryans yelled (mind you, with his dick still out). "You just tazed a pregnant woman in the stomach!"

Even the normally disaffected Tits could not help but raise an objection to the captain's conduct. "You're *torturing* her! You can't taser a pregnant woman in the stomach!"

Straker's wide eyes shot to the very well-endowed girl. "I hate to tell you this, missy, but I just did!" And then, wouldn't you know it, he re-aimed his weapon and—

PAP!

—put two darts into Tits' big knocked-up-prisoner belly.

I don't find it worthwhile to describe the effect for it would simple be a "rehash" of Bigfoot's experience, and a superfluous use of space.

For some reason, Ryans *still* had not put his dick back in his pants. Likewise, was not happy with his summation that old Captain Straker had finally gone off the deep end.

Then:

"Oh, why not?" Straker said to himself with a laugh and pressed the reactivate button on the right of the weapon, which sent another 50,000 volts into each prisoner's belly. Now the two inmates were *really* rockin' and rollin', and their screams made Ryans' ears hurt.

"Fuckin' A, Captain! Are you nuts? You're gonna make the kids come out!"

"What's that?"

"You'll make 'em have miscarriages!" Ryans bellowed over the screams and crackling. "There'll be fetuses and placentas and shit all over the fuckin' place!"

After the next five-second jolt of agony, Tits and Bigfoot fell silent but their violent convulsions continued in what was—I regret to say—an entertaining spectacle, instigated by the Taser's ability to disrupt the central nervous system via what's known as "psychomotor agitation." Poor Bigfoot's breasts flopped as if she were sitting on a jackhammer. Perhaps it is relevant to mention (or perhaps not) that the brisk electrocution of both women caused their milk-filled breasts to leak profusely. This made for an interesting effect.

The Captain really did seem to be in a psychotic state now. He acted like he hadn't heard Ryans at all as he took a few steps toward Bo Peep, and then he said, "I've always believed in fair play, and *equal* opportunity. So I think it's only fair that I taser you in the stomach too," and then he raised the device before the terrified girl. "Wouldn't be right for those other two to have all the fun, huh?"

Keep in mind, now, that the taser nodes sunk into the bellies of Tits and Bigfoot remained connected to their leads, and what you must understand is that Straker brandished what is called a Taser X3, which accommodated not one, not two, but, yes, *three* dart cartridges all in the same unit. In other words, three individuals could be tortured at the same time—all in the name, of course, of law and order.

Bo Peep shuddered in her seat as the good Captain gave her breasts a squeeze or two (or maybe three) and then pulled her orange gown up over the swollen white belly. Straker chuckled when he said, "I wouldn't want you to feel left out," and he raised the taser point blank.

The inmate urinated involuntarily, and was barely audible when she blubbered, "Please, mister captain, please no, don't taser me. Fuck! All I did was shoplift a can of Vienna sausages at Dollar General, and then the cops planted that crack on me..."

"Aw, ain't that a shame..."

And here's what happened next:

We'll pause here for an aside. The great film maker Alfred Hitchcock once very profoundly explained the importance of the different between "shock" and "suspense." Two people sit at a table, talking. A bomb under the table explodes without foreshadow, and the audience is jolted by the shock of it, but that shock will seem of no consequence a moment later. However when the director *shows* the bomb first and lets the audience know it's there, then *suspense* is created, and this suspense imparts a more entertaining movie-going experience. In other words, taking the time to build suspense is the right way to tell a story, while resorting merely to uncrafted shock is the wrong way; indeed, the *cheap* way. Therefore, we will utilize the *cheap* way in this particular circumstance.

In a split-second, everything jerked around, the female inmates screamed, and Straker and Ryans were slammed down as the bus was tipped over on its side with a ferocious BANG!

The right side of the bus was now the ceiling, and from that ceiling all three of our gravid inmates hung suspended from the chains cuffed to their hands, all understandably screaming. Ryans landed in a seat on the left side of the bus, and suffered temporarily from a smack to the head and a discombobulation of his sense of orientation. His penis was still out, by the way, and given the position he was in (on his back and legs folded over) and given the fact that it was a penis *larger* than average size...the "glans" was nearly in his mouth.

"What the fuck was that!" yelled Captain Straker, now folded over himself in a left-hand seat. "Did ya park on the fuckin' train tracks, Ryans!?"

But there were no train tracks, and no intersecting roads, so what exactly *did* happen? Ryans gathered his senses, awkwardly stood up, and looked around. The three inmates continued to shriek in horror, hanging by their right arms, kicking and flailing their legs in mid-air. Ryans thought of pregnant pinatas. He tried to step his way toward the front of the bus, to get to the radio, and he had to push each girl aside to do so (as if they were sides of beef which, kind of, they were) but before he got all the way to the front...

He stood and stared.

"What the fuck am I seeing?"

If he'd had time for further pondering, he'd consider hallucination from the smack on the head, but, lo, there was no time for that, for the "thing" he thought he'd seen kneeling outside the now perpendicular windshield seemed to be examining the inside of the bus with one eye nearly the size of a croquet ball, and the other the size of a marble. Whatever it was, its head was huge, lop-sided, and bald, and it wore no manner of garment. It seemed to be all hunched over as it peered in, all bunched muscles and weird pallid skin with liver spots or something. Additionally—and even *more* notably than the fact that the thing must be at least eight feet tall when standing upright—there was a great roll of something between its legs like a curled tube of spoiled dough, the width of the fat end of a ball bat. Could it be...the thing's...*penis?*

The windshield imploded with a nudge of the visitor's hand; it rained safety glass. Ever the steward of law and order, Sergeant Ryans (in spite of having just defecated in his pants) hit the thumb-snap of his holster, shucked his nine-millimeter, and squeezed off three perfect double-taps into the thing's center of mass.

If that didn't do it, NOTHIN' will, Ryans thought with some pride, but regrettably, for him, *that* didn't do it. Ryans could see the butts of his hollow-point slugs actually *sticking out* of the thing's massive chest muscles.

Then its equally massive arm shot forward in a preposterous reach, snatched Ryans by the neck, and pulled him forward. There was no time to scream. If you can imagine Ryans as a sheet of paper, that's pretty much what he was rolled up like in the monstrous hands of this inhuman perpetrator. Of course, Ryans didn't crinkle as paper would, but he sure did *crackle* as most of his bones were effortlessly broken.

And in case you're wondering:

Yes. Sergeant Ryans' penis was still out at the moment of his death, and when his adversary noticed this, it snapped that penis and scrotum right off and swallowed it whole.

Why not?

Now came insane Caption Straker's turn to step up. In this new psychotic state he surprisingly experienced no fear at being trapped in a prison bus with a naked stink-reeking monster that was so big it couldn't stand up.

"Whatever the fuck you are," spoke the captain, "you picked the wrong guy to fuck with today, and before I fill you full of nine mill, I'm gonna spark you up a tad."

If you'll recall, Straker still had one unexpended cartridge in his taser, and this he aimed at the…the thing. Remember, too, that the first two sets of darts remained still connected by their leads into the distended bellies of the now dangling and traumatized Bigfoot and Tits, and Straker hit the reactivation button just to make sure everything was still in operating order. Amid the electric crackling, both unfortunate young ladies flipped and flopped on the ends of their chains and screamed to wake the hackneyed dead, peeing, pooping, and vomiting in quite a unique spectacle.

When the five-second discharge had ended, Straker grinned at his visitor. "See that, buster? That's what I'm gonna do to you in about two seconds." He looked approvingly at the bulky yellow non-lethal weapon (non-lethal, the authorities claimed, yet tasers to date had killed at least forty-nine people—mostly criminal scum, but still…)

The validity of his threat was doubtful (as would we all will reasonably expect) but Captain Straker lined up the two red laser dots on his target and—

PAP!

—fired.

The top dart stuck into the tube of rolled flesh between the trespasser's massive legs, while the second sunk right smack dab into one of the avocado-sized lumps (presumably the creature's testicles) just below that region.

"Right in the dick!" Straker celebrated.

And the five-second discharge of 50,000 volts buzzed directly into the "meat and potatoes," so to speak, of the monster's "junk."

Well, this may have "sparked" the creature "up a tad," but not in the way Captain Straker had hoped. The flaccid appendage of flesh that had taken the first dart sprang to full erection—at least a foot and a half in length, with dark veins fat as bloodsuckers pulsing beneath the mottled, ill-yellow penile skin. If the creature could smile, it did, or at least it made some facial gesture to indicate pleasure from all that electricity surging into the most nerve-crammed parts of its body.

At the finish of the five-second charge (as you may have already guessed), orgasm ensued, one gout of sperm after the next pumping from that inhumanly large erection. One spurt actually hit Straker in the chest, so far was its range, and another—yes!—hit him in the face. Stupefied and sperm-faced, Straker shucked his Glock but...not fast enough.

The captain was knocked down at once like a fat, uniformed bowling pin as the thing flung Ryans' crumpled up and penis-less dead body at him with the force of, say, a 100 mph fastball.

WHAP!

The detention officer was folded over one of the seats, and bones were heard cracking. It would have been his good fortune to have broken his back or neck, but it was only his hips that were spectacularly fractured. Straker bellowed inarticulate words like "Arrg!" and "Bleck!" and "Futhermucker fuck shit!"

Well said!

The thing, monster, troll, demon, whatever it was, kneed itself forward in an attitude of acute inquisitiveness. Then it pulled down Captain Straker's pants...

***

By now, most of the Bighead's superior brain function had returned with all that gray-matter than had regrown inside his skull; in fact, some of that tissue had even ventured *out* of the big hole in the back of his skull. He could remember everything now, and it occurred to him that he was now possessed of even more awareness, intuition, intelligence, etc. than he'd ever had.

Well, let me clarify. For instance, with everything the Bighead now knew, he didn't know what a Whitman's Sampler was but if he had, that's what he might have regarded this little gray bus as. He was having a jolly time, and a jollier time it would be in the following moments.

Intuition, yes, and simple observation made the function of the funny looking gun (the taser) more than plain. See, the fat detention officer plainly wore a *second* such weapon on his belt, and this the

Bighead withdrew in the next moment. He squeezed the trigger three times—

PAP! PAP! PAP!

—and planted three sets of electrified darts into the fat man's exposed genitals. The Bighead watching the man convulsing and listening to the man's excruciating screams might be likened to a five-year-old boy's captivation of watching his first electric train set choo-choo around the track in wide-eyed wonder. After the first five seconds, the Bighead naturally pushed the reactivation button for further entertainment, and this he did a number of times until the battery of the device went dead. It will be added, too, that Captain Straker stroked out during that last buzz from the taser.

Had the Bighead been well-versed in the English language, he probably would've thought something like: *Wow!* or *Neat-o!*

Ah, but there remained that first three-shot taser. Bighead yanked out the pair of darts from his own genitals, then faced the two women into whose bellies the other darts had been deftly sunk. Both women, of course, still dangled from the metal fetters about their wrists, and one—the prettier of the two—appeared to be unconscious. The other—the bigger one—lolled and turned on her chain, staring at the Bighead with hemorrhaged eyes. "Aw, fuck," she grunted. "What a fucked up day..."

This couldn't have been more true for either young lady, and the Bighead discerned no good reason the day should not get even more *fucked up* for them. He picked up that first taser and—will you be shocked to hear it?—he pressed the reactivation button on this one too, and *continued* doing so until the weapon was totally drained of power. Superfluous words need not be expended on the sounds the inmates made, nor on the particulars of their death throes. At the end, the fetuses of both women had been miscarried. First, the babies dangled from their mothers by their umbilical cords, and then—

SPLAP!

—they fell out fully along with the placentas (or might it be plancenti? No, I see not, thanks to this invention called a spellchecker). It was quite the glistening, gory mess that Sergeant

Ryans had postulated, and I will not burden the reader with details describing exactly how these poor fetuses and placentas wound up in the Bighead's "bread basket." But as is the case with anyone who scarfs down a big meal, the Bighead needed something to wash this one down with.

Whether or not the two girls were now dead hardly mattered; the Bighead was not fussy about such things. One nipple at a time, his superhuman suction drained the mammary glands of both women at a rate of about a second per tit, and those big sloshy milk-filled honkers were *dead empty* and *bone dry*. He glanced around the cramped quarters and assayed his handiwork: belly full, cock limp and still buzzing from that great nut, and everyone dead or soon would be. The Whitman's Sampler, indeed, was done.

Or…was it?

He turned around on his monstrous knees (getting a bit aggravated that he could not stand up in this tipped-over metal box). Something pecked at him, a notion or feeling, but what?

Who knew? Maybe the Bighead was claustrophobic.

But lo and behold, one treat remained—the least conspicuous of the three hanging women. Bighead had scarcely noticed her but now he became aware of her unique appearance when compared to the other two. She was the skinniest little thing, yet that skinniness visually clashed with the *big giant paper white belly* bulging from her lean frame. Here was likely the best candy in the entire sampler. Stuffed inside this wan little creature was a baby quivering with fresh new blood and flesh, and it would no doubt taste ambrosial; it would be like the difference between chicken livers and the butter-fried liver of force-fed Toulouse geese (not that the Bighead knew what any of that stuff was! This comparison is just another lugubrious example of an undisciplined novelist's indulgence).

And here is another one. When the Bighead opened his huge yellowish hand with fat green-brown veins pulsing beneath the skin, he could actually "palm" the entire belly the way, say, Lebron James could palm a fuckin' basketball, and I must add that the distraught girl's belly was even *bigger* than a regulation basketball. If Bighead were to squeeze this delightful while protuberance, he knew that delectable, very fresh baby inside would spill right out along with all the fixin's. It might even be said that a bit of adoration seemed present in the way the Bighead caressed the stomach.

The girl's terrified and flabbergasted eyes met his, and she whimpered, "Puh-please, Mr. Monster. Don't eat my baby. Fuck, I swear I wouldn't even be here if I hadn't gotten knocked up by a john and then stole a can of fuckin' Vienna sausages. I was starving! I mean, have you ever *eaten* Vienna sausages? They taste like crap. Only bums eat 'em!" And then, as might be expected, she broke into another round of fitful, blubbering sobs.

In the recent regrowth of his brain, the Bighead understood some the gist of the language here, but he didn't know what the fuck she was talking about. He wanted out of this tin can; he had things to do. So he crawled back out the front of the bus and, no, he didn't eat the baby—he was *stuffed*—and he didn't kill the girl because, well, he thought she was kind of cute.

Outside, he stood back up to his full height of nearly nine feet, burped, looked at the sky with some semblance of satisfaction, and then continued on his way.

From the bus, the skinny girl could be heard gushing, "Oh, thank you! Thank you, Mr. Monster! God bless you!"

The Bighead heard these words. He paused, blinked, then kept moving on. He didn't know who God was, and couldn't imagine why someone he didn't know would want to bless him!

***

At the onset, the prospect of finding the grave of Ephriam Crafter seemed to exist at a very low order level of possibility. The grounds were wildly overgrown, and even in the ancient fenced-in graveyard, there were few tombstones and no vaults, mostly just stone markers flush with the ground whose inscriptions were obscured by brown weeds. "This'll take forever," said the Writer. "It might be a good idea to go back to town and buy a lawnmower. Can't read any of these names."

Dawn's big tits stood out grandly beneath her tight t-shirt. "I wouldn't be surprised if my old boss Mr. Winter-Damon buried Crafter without a marker, and pocketed the money."

The American Way, thought the Writer.

The woods that ringed the hilltop property whispered around them from a sudden breeze. Overhead, birds cavorted amongst lush green branches. The sun shimmered down. All in all, it made for a beautiful day to vandalize a grave.

"I don't think we'll need the mower," said the black-clothed Case. He stood just away from the others, looking down. "I think it's right about here."

Dawn immediately knelt at the spot. "No marker. What makes you think the grave is here?"

Case shrugged. "The same thing that makes me think you had two dollar-store-brand Pop Tarts for breakfast this morning. The cinnamon kind, right?"

Dawn looked up with astonishment. "How the fuck did you know what?"

Case winced. "Profanity is the devil's stain upon all language. It's not necessary. All cussing does is injure your friendship with God."

But all this the Writer found very curious and, for some reason, credible. "So you're psychic," he said.

"You might call it that," said Case. "Second sight, whatever. It's no big deal, just a little tidbit God threw me when I gave my life to Him. That's why I work for the Diocese. I make myself of use to them, and to God."

"Another Holy Roller!" Snowie delighted. "Just like Pastor Tommy!"

"Funny you should mention him. Early this morning I checked into a local hotel, and discovered that Pastor Ignatius is staying there as well."

"The Due Drop In?" Dawn asked.

Why, yes.

"That's where me'n my ma work!" Snowie said with some zeal.

"Oh, yeah," Case said, "I see the resemblance easily now," which could mean the facial resemblance or the resemblance in their drop-dead stellar brick shit-house tits, or of course the albinism. "As a matter of fact, I invited the pastor up here, to help me snoop around. Got to admit, I was a bit star struck—he's quite famous."

The Writer and the girls chose not to make the obvious revelation regarding gummy worms and kiddie porn. *How psychic can Case really be?* "Well, all this talk of psychic ability has me very interested, and I can't think of a better way to test it than this..." He handed Dawn the shovel. "Start digging, Dawn. Unless you *don't* want that new car."

Dawn frowned, then shrugged. "I've dug up graves in Iraq, Afghanistan, and Sierra Leone, so I guess I can dig one up here. But it's so damn *hot!*" With this recognition, she once again removed her t-shirt, brandishing those bare mammarian beauties. Snowie, of course, followed suit, an act to which the Writer found no objection. *Tits never get old...*

But as Dawn removed the first shovelful of earth, Case frowned. "I don't get it," he said to the Writer. "We can't let a woman dig a grave. Is there no chivalry left in the world?"

"Not here. One thing my old fat ass is *not* doing today is digging up a grave," the Writer told him. "Dawn's being punished anyway, aren't you, Dawn? For saying mean things to Snowie."

Case took off his black dress shirt. "I'd be happy to dig."

"What a gentleman!" Dawn said and gave him the shovel, but then she paused, staring. "What...what happened?"

She was referring to a strange and overtly obvious patchwork of scarring over much of Case's bare arms and chest. It didn't quite look like old burns, but something worse.

"Oh, that," the man said, muscles flexing as he began to dig. "The short version is this: before God showed me the Light, I was an abominable sinner, and I did...*horrifying* things. I'm trying to atone for all that now. But back then, ten years ago or so, I was covered with tattoos, mostly prison tatts. The only legitimate art is art that praises God but, believe me, these tattoos *didn't* do that. So I cut them off." This last sentence was added matter-of-factly, as if of no importance. Then he kept digging.

"Wow," Dawn whispered. "That's hardcore as fuck! I'm soaking!"

Next, Snowie volunteered some cheerful and eloquently stated information. "I gotta fuckin' pee again, I'm a fuckin' *peein' machine,* I is!" Then she trotted off to the woods to do her business.

Case continued to dig in a manner that seemed effortless; he'd already gotten a foot deep. He looked up at the Writer who was craning his neck in efforts to see Snowie void her bladder. *Okay. So what? I'm a bit of a pervert.* And she implemented an interesting diversity; instead of squatting with her pants down, she lay on her back, pushed her pants to her ankles, and hugged her knees, releasing her urine in an upward arch, like a water fountain with too much pressure in the line.

Oh, but there I go again: burdening you with imagery that's wholly unnecessary! Call it an old writer's indulgence...

"Someone once told me," Case began, still digging, "that graves were really four feet deep instead of six."

"That's true in most cases," Dawn said. The sweat on her bare breasts made for a near-blinding display. "And the caskets are typically two feet high, so you should only have to dig about two feet to get to the top, or a little less if the coffin's inside a burial liner."

The next push of the shovel verified this data. "Here's the top," Case said. He scraped the shovel-edge against a curved sheet of shiny gray metal, and in only another few minutes, the man had excavated the entirety of the lid.

"I am duly impressed, sir," said the Writer. "Not only with the efficacy of your digging skills but also by your now-undoubted psychic inclinations."

"It's really true," Dawn said in a wide-eyed hush. "The body of Ephriam Crafter, buried by two rednecks my boss hired years ago."

The Writer was about to interject the query of what to do next but this was interrupted by Snowie, who'd pulled her pants back up and scampered topless back to the group. "Hey, yawl! Lookit what I found!"

In her hand was a rectangular board of some kind. She presented the object to the others, holding it just under her staggeringly gorgeous breasts.

"See? 'Tis a wee-gee board! Bet it's the same one the Cubbler Twins used back when they come up here on Halloween! Let's use it! Let's ask it questions!"

Dawn smirked. "Snowie, you use that thing and tomorrow morning you'll be giving birth to fifty-pounds of satanic shit."

Snowie's lips formed into a hesitant "o." "O-oh, yeah, guess you're right. I shore wouldn't want none'a that..."

"I'd put that aside if I were you," Case advised. "All those things do is solicit the devil and invite ungodliness into the lives of those who use it."

The Writer didn't know exactly how he felt about this notion, but, *I don't want Captain Howdy going home with us later.* "Let's forget about the Ouija board and concentrate on...Well, I'm not sure what now."

"Yeah," Case said. "Now that we got Crafter's coffin, what's the next step? Open it? Then what?"

The Writer scratched his beard.

"You can trust me on this, if it's your plan to get the casket out of the ground, it's not gonna be easy," Dawn said. "The lock mechanism is probably rusted, and roots and shit have probably grown into the box. So, whatever it is you want to do, we should do it soon because, after all, this is broad daylight. Someone could see us—a cop for instance, 'cos the car is parked at the entrance. And didn't you say something about Pastor Tommy coming here too? What are you gonna tell him when he sees you've dug up someone's grave?"

These were excellent questions, and the Writer was ashamed of himself for not having previously thought of them.

But, wouldn't you know it?

At that moment, his cellphone plipped—a text message.

"Who on earth could this be?" he said and extracted the heinously expensive device that he hated. The text log read NO NUMBER. "No surprise there," said the Writer more to himself. "It's my doppelganger."

"Your *what?*" Case asked.

"Never mind."

The text message read "Have the two bimbos use the board," but when he texted back "Why?" the DELIVERY FAILED notice popped up.

"Dawn, Snowie, please don't ask why," the Writer ordered. "But it will be worth your time to make use of that Ouija board."

"Shore!" Snowie said, while Dawn replied simultaneously, "No fuckin' way!"

"What's this all about?" Case asked, leaning on the shovel, his scarred arms and chest shiny in sweat. "Doppelganger?"

"You wouldn't believe me if I told you, and I'm not even sure I believe it myself. And, Dawn, please don't make difficulties. There's five hundred in it for both of you."

Dawn answered, "No fuckin'...Five hundred? I'm in."

"But there's no, you know, the thingie they use," Snowie observed.

"I believe it's call a planchette," the Writer said, "but the proper attitude, I think, is the most important component. A coin, for instance, should suffice?" He handed Snowie a quarter.

"Just let it be noted that I strongly advise against this," Case said. "It doesn't matter to me because I'm protected. But I don't know about you guys."

"What do you mean, protected?"

"I'm protected by God, the Father Almighty," Case calmly said. "Nothing conjured from that board can hurt me. I hope the same is true for you, but..." He shrugged.

But neither Dawn nor Snowie were hearing this advice, for five hundred reasons each. In seconds, both young ladies—if you could call them that—were sitting beside the opened grave, the board betwixt them, one finger of each of their hands lightly touching the quarter, and...tits out. It was a curious display and one of which the Writer had never heard: a Topless Ouija Board Session.

"I'm gonna dig a gouge down this side, to expose the edge of the lid," Case informed, and began digging again. "But I doubt we can pop the top open with this shovel. See if you can find a crow bar or something, maybe a claw hammer."

The Writer nodded, half-jogging back to the house (*half* was all he could manage today). He searched "high and low," as I believe the proper saying goes, but as might be expected in such a house, no hammers, crow bars, or the like were found. He *did* discover, however, a sterling silver pie server decorated with beautiful scroll work and imprinted with the marker's mark PAUL REVERE & SONS, 1791.

He hefted it in his hand, a sturdy, well-made tool. However priceless, he thought it very likely to succeed in defeating the lock of Crafter's casket. But when he returned to the very untoward scene outside—

Oh, dear. What's the big to-do now?

Dawn and Snowie, still sitting on the ground and facing each other, seemed to be...*growling* at each other. Hackneyed as it may sound, they were both baring teeth that appeared to be anything but their normal teeth but were instead tiny greenish-white objects pointed as if sharpened. And, too, their necks were painfully craned, showing stout blue veins, while their wide-opened eyes showed no hint of pupils or irises, just white.

"What the hell's this?" the Writer shouted.

"I told them not to fool around with that thing!" Case yelled back.

Thunder clapped hard overhead, in spite of a complete absence of clouds, and there seemed to be a rumbling from below ground. In between the rumbles emerged a dark muttering, which struck one as of some macabre manner of *speech.*

"They're both possessed!" Case stated the obvious.

The awesome bare breasts of each woman began to *shiver* and now their eyes were showing only black. The molested words from below-ground issued louder and with more urgency, something like: "*Glub nb nub grlm nabbl e uh nurlethitep,*" and then Dawn barked more familiar words: "*Negotium perambulans in tenebris,*" and lastly, Snowie burped, hitched, and then—

"Woe-dobbin!" exclaimed the Writer.

Snowie projectile-vomited a hard and perfectly straight plume of bile directly into the snarling face of Dawn, who then responded in kind and—

"Errrrrrrrrrrrrp!"

—blew one right back into Snowie's face.

Several seconds of silence passed, then the Writer looked at Case and remarked, "Wow."

"Wow is right," the newcomer said. "Those girls were possessed."

"Evidently so," the Writer replied.

"And it's your fault."

The Writer frowned, roused to object, but then just said, "I know."

Both women now lay unconscious in separate heaps on either side of the vomit-slicked board. Case stepped before them, raised a small pocket Bible over his head, and said, "God, by Your name save us, and by Your might defend this cause and hear my prayer, I beg of Thee to hearken to the words of my mouth, o Lord." Now he looked down at the two still girls. "Unclean spirits, heed my words, and depart from these two servants of the Heavenly Father, in the name of God the Father and of His only son our Savior Jesus Christ the Righteous, and of the Holy Ghost, I commandeth thee—be gone."

As the last word was spoken, both girls spasmed once, screamed, then sat bolt upright in the grass, bewildered.

"Really?" asked the Writer. "Exorcism is that easy?"

"Most of the time, sure, because most of the time the demonic spirits are small-time, chump-change, like these here. Lucifer saves the big Mack Daddies for folks far more important than us. To him, we're small potatoes."

"What the FUCK!" Dawn yelled, and Snowie chimed in, "What the hell happened? We're covered in puke!"

"Long story short," said the Writer, "the Quija board summoned two demon spirits that possessed you, made you throw up on each other, and then Case performed a convenience-store-type exorcism."

The women looked at each other, mouths (and bare breasts) hanging.

"I was inclined to believe that the board might shed some light on exactly what we're supposed to do with Crafter's body now that it's been exhumed, but I'm afraid nothing of the sort occurred. Now do us all a favor and go in the house and wash that vomit off yourselves. See if the shower works." The Writer sniffed. "It smells awful...like stomach acid and Pop Tarts." The revulsion had finally set in; Snowie and Dawn scrambled into the house like large-breasted madwomen.

119

"Not quite sure what to do next," Case remarked. "But..."

Crack!

Case inserted the priceless pie-server under the lip of the coffin lid, jerked it upward, and the lid popped open.

"Dawn said that Crafter's body was embalmed by her boss," the Writer contributed, "and I don't know if that means toxic gases could accumulate after all this time. Therefore...be careful."

Case shrugged. "If I'm gonna kick the bucket from toxic gases in a coffin, then it's God's will...I think." He leaned over again, and lifted up the coffin's lid. The hinges creaked wonderfully, which made for an appropriate embellishment for the event.

Nothing in the way of toxic gases was evident; in fact, the Writer noticed no smell at all, good or bad. Yet he had to admit, when he walked around the other side of the unearthed grave, he did so with more than a little trepidation.

Even embalmed, what would the corpse look like after all these years of entombment?

The Writer peeked around...

"Looks in great shape," Case remarked. "Except for the complexion."

It was an accurate assessment, the Writer now saw. Had the image been seen in black and white instead of "living" color, it would have been that of a well-dressed elderly man with a gray Van Dyke and longish hair, lying asleep.

"Nice threads," Case said.

"Armani, I do believe, but the maroon tie doesn't quite work for me."

"And the skin-tone, of course. Looks sort of like...what's that kind of cheese? Muenster?"

"Right. With those little crevices in it."

But now both men scratched their heads. They'd done what they'd set out to do: exhume Crafter's body. "What do you suppose we're supposed to do now?" Case made the inquiry.

The Writer felt gypped. "Well, I had it on, shall we say, a competent authority that the Ouija board would answer that question, but we both saw what came of that."

"Wait," Case uttered. He was looking queerly back at the

vomited-slopped board in the grass. "Do you...see that?"

The Writer peered over, was about to reply in the negative, but then a genuine chill crawled up his spine.

Some...anomalous activity seemed to be taking place on the surface of the vomit-sheened spirit board...

"What *is* that?" one or both of them said.

Putting the reader in visual grasp of what needs to be understood requires the pen of a Shakespeare or a Dickens, and *this* author—believe me—wields no such a pen. But I will do the best I can.

Imagine, if you will, a standard Hasbro-brand Ouija Board, but such a one that is covered almost entirely with pale, ill-colored vomit (bile, mostly, with not much in the way of "chunks"). Now, after constructing this unlikely picture in your mind, I ask you to additionally imagine that an *invisible person* is perched before the board and, with an equally invisible index finger, is calmly and deliberately drawing circles in the vomit.

Are you following me thus far?

Just as it occurs to both men what is taking place, the man known as the Writer utters an uncouth "Holy ever-living *fuck,*" and the black man frowns at the reckless misuse of our wonderful English language.

"You're seeing this, right?" says Case.

"Fuck yes," says the Writer.

The agency utilizing this invisible finger made four circles on the slimy board, then stopped. Neither spectator needed to squint very much to see that the finger marks had encircled four of the letters of the alphabet on the board's surface. The letter were thus:

A, B, C, K.

Had this circumstance suddenly become and supernatural version of Scrabble?

"Correct me if I'm wrong," said the Writer, "but there's only one word that could spell."

"Back."

An interesting puzzle. "But in what context? Maybe it means we should go back in the house. Or go back home."

Case blinked. "No, no." He walked to Crafter's stiff corpse in the open casket. "I just got a jolt same as I got when we were looking for the grave. I think it means there's something on Crafter's back."

The Writer considered this prospect. *I'm glad the board didn't spell backSIDE...*

"For thousands of years," Case explained, "necromancers and sorceresses saw to it that they were buried with something of occult significance: a piece of writing, a potion, an amulet, whatever. Something to be found later, particularly by someone who knew to look for it. Some of the witches of Loudun had swallowed sealed vials of poison before they were hanged, and the vials were later recovered by their apprentices and used against their persecutors. Also, tinctures and powders to inflict curses and simply bad luck, powerful sigils that summon devils, stuff like that. Maps were also a favorite thing to be buried on or in witches and warlocks."

At this point, Case bent over at the side of the grave, and with a dexterity that was surprising, flipped Crafter's cadaver over with a light *flup,* and with no hesitation whatsoever, squatted right down into the grave. He pulled up Crafter's collar and, with one of those illegal "flick-it" pocket knives, he—yes—cut the suit jacket and the dress shirt straight down the middle of the back.

"And behind curtain number one is..." the Writer said, but it really wasn't the least bit funny.

Case parted the deteriorating fabric on Crafter's back, indeed, like two curtains. And what was revealed on the cheesy skin of the dead man's back?

"Some kind of tattoo, I suppose," the Writer ventured.

Yes, but crudely executed and clearly *not* the work of a formidable artist. More akin to the crayon work of a child. Irregular columns of words existed on either side of the drawing. What that drawing depicted with be described momentarily. The words, however, must be noted immediately.

They were words that appeared to be written in no language the Writer had ever seen.

Or...

Had he?

Next, familiarity slapped him "upside" the head, as I believe the saying goes, and Case seemed touched by some familiarity as well. He said, "This looks like part of the Voy—"

"The Voynich Manuscript of the mid-1400's," finished the Writer. "The only book on earth that cannot be read, because it was penned in an unknown language."

Case looked at him askance. "You know about the Voynich?"

"Yes, I very much do, and if you'll pardon me a moment, I'll elaborate." Here, the Writer hastily departed the scene, returned to the house, and extricated the Voynich page (page 238) that he'd discovered—along with the Webley revolver and the Hand of Glory—when he'd first searched beneath the El Camino's bench seat. Less than a minute's time had him back to the site of the opened grave, whereupon he passed the ultra-rare sheet of vellum to the black-clad black man, whose eyes immediately widened with unreserved incredulity.

"How on earth did you get *this*? This is *priceless!*"

The Writer shrugged. "I found it under the seat of my car. I believe it was pilfered from Crafter's house over twenty years ago by two local miscreants, namely Dickey Caudill and Balls Conner. And also, possibly, by a third person who…may have been myself."

Case shot him a funky look. "Say again?"

"I had a catastrophic case of amnesia," the Writer said rather lugubriously. "I was in Luntville over twenty years ago, and I'm pretty sure I was at this house, but I don't remember any of it." He sighed. "Long story, doesn't matter. But, yes, I'm certain that's an original Voynich page, procured somehow by Ephraim Crafter for what could only be *occult* purposes."

Case studied the sheet. "This is from one of the gatefold sections; a larger sheet of vellum was folded over twice, creating actually four pages on each side, then the entire gatefold was quired into the book itself."

"And the experts say that at least thirty pages were stolen over the centuries," the Writer contributed.

Case appeared in a mild shock. "I know"—he gulped—"and this is one of them."

"The original manuscript is at Yale now, and it's been digitalized entirely. Maybe we could go online and figure out what other page this corresponds to—"

An excitement suddenly glinted in Case's eyes. "I...don't think we have to..."

They both looked down at the "tattoo" on the corpse's back. Both men lowered themselves to one knee, the Writer doing so with much more difficulty than his partner had, and then he said, "You're absolutely right!"

This word-painting business can be a vexing activity at times, especially when the author must describe a "picture in a picture" sort of situation: the characters are looking at a picture, drawing, etching, what have you, and the reader must believe what the author tells them they are seeing. They are looking, in this case, at an old sheet of vellum with a drawing on it, and then they are looking at a drawing on a dead man's back. Describing this in a coherent way, and in a way that makes the reader see what the characters are seeing...can become quite convoluted at times; hence, the convoluted paragraph I've just written. However, *this* author is no *ordinary* writer, and he will do what he can.

The upper half of the Writer's sheet of vellum (if you can carry your mind back to Part One of this awkwardly executed saga) was filled by an irregular block of undecipherable hand-writing. But the bottom half of the sheet contained a drawing, and an odd one at that: naked female figures, apparently some months pregnant, wading thigh-deep in a pool of some green liquid. All of the women depicted are looking to the left of the page (indeed, almost as if they are peering at something on a previous page, but a page that doesn't exist.)

Also, from the left side of the pool snakes a tube (or might it be a hose?) which extends off the page.

Our protagonist Writer held this sheet of vellum immediately adjacent to the "tattoo" on Crafter's embalmed back. As you've likely already surmised, the "tube" leading out of the green pool on the vellum seemed to connect in exact proportions to an identical tube drawn on the old warlock's back. In other words, the vellum illustration and the illustration on Crafter's back were part of the same illustration.

Wait a minute! Did I just hear a reader out there yell "This is boring! And what the hell is vellum?" Ah, I do believe I did. Vellum, my friend, is calfskin or pigskin especially treated for writing material, the historic intermediary between papyrus and paper. As for this book being boring, I'll only suggest that you are picky and very difficult to please!

Now, where was I? Yes! You're wondering what is depicted in the stylistically identical illustration on Crafter's Muenster-cheese back, and it was just this:

Another crudely drawn figure stood mid-page, this one male, a horned demon standing with taloned hands and feet, a pronged tail, a fanged grin; evidently also the recipient of some libidinal excitement, because sprouting from the apex of its corded, muscular legs was a hideously veined erection of some considerable length. This appalling effigy seemed at home in such a tome as this, but, odder still, and perhaps even more appalling, was what indubitably extended from the demonic penis: a hose or tube of some kind. It was a green, and it snaked away from the erection, traveling off the page where it connected precisely to the tube on the other page, the Writer's physical vellum page, and it ended in the green pool of naked women all glancing to the left.

The Writer's vision seemed to blur as he examined the absurd artwork. "Tell me if I've got this right. What we've got here is the devil with a tube connected to his boner, and the tube empties into the pool of badly drawn naked pregnant women. Is *that* what this is?"

"Yeah," Case said. "Sure looks like it to me."

"So what's it supposed to mean? Is it allegorical? Is it some kind of occult symbology? The devil dispensing his semen to the women of the world?"

Case frowned. "I don't know what it means. It probably doesn't mean anything, it's probably just some 15th century whackjob's perverted drawing. I'm far more interested in what's on the rest of the page. Looks familiar, doesn't it?"

The Writer, not always the most observant man in the crowd, stared higher at Crafter's back. Nothing registered. Depicted there in the artist's crude style were several arched doorways, made of brick or stone. Another naked pregnant woman was pointing to the doorway on the left. This door was closed and clearly it was fashioned from wooden planks. Jutting from the center planks was what appeared to be a bloody spike, and impaled on the spike was what appeared to be a human heart, but the artist's skills were so amateurish, he couldn't be sure. But there were five more doors in a row next to it, and they were all open and showing plumes of flame.

The Writer looked a moment more, then—

Wham!

"Holy shit! Those look like the doorways in Crafter's basement!"

"Uh-huh, the Traversion Bridles, and there are six of them, just like there are six here in this lousy drawing." Case looked at the Writer. "We need to investigate this more closely...in the basement."

The prospect of returning to the basement—now—was not one to which the Writer looked forward with any enthusiasm. *But this is what I'm here to do. I have a feeling it's my destiny...* "You're right, and we're gonna need the diagram on Crafter's back for further reference."

"Yeah, but I'm *not* dragging that old man's corpse down there, Church work or not," said Case.

Church work, thought the Writer with some levity, for he was staring at a dead body in a plundered grave. "I'll just take a picture of his back with my cellphone," the Writer said, and this he did with an undue amount of fiddling.

Then they departed for the house, leaving the opened grave as it was, determining to fill it back in later.

This was a *colossal* mistake.

***

As this second leg of our backwoods journey nears its end, I must notify the reader that the final sequences of events take place with considerable speed; therefore I must bid you to be as attentive as possible. Be reminded that much has taken place until now, such that I believe it advisable for me to utilize what I've always thought of as the Charles L. Grant Technique, named for the late great award-winning author of those wonderful old Oxrun Station books of the '70s. The technique involves, in a serviceable way, a refreshing of the reader's memory to past details before the story's climax ensues.

1. Snowie and Dawn, nowhere to be seen at this moment, have navigated themselves somewhere into the depths of the house, in order that they might wash themselves after having been slopped up by apparently *demonic* vomit in a mishap with the Ouija board. Our two shapely female leads, in fact, are at this very moment taking a shower—together—in one of many bathrooms. And as much as the author would thrill to describe their mutual activities in said shower, I decline the opportunity in the consideration of space.

2. You'll recall the previously mentioned, but little-seen, Pastor Tommy Ignatius, who, in Part One of this befuddled journey was observed via closed-circuit spy camera—just last night, mind you—watching child pornography on his laptop computer whilst masturbating. His masturbation was augmented by his inserting several pieces of candy known as "gummy worms"...into his, um, urethra. In other words, Pastor Tommy is a howling fraud as a religious spokesman, but that's really nothing new these days, is it? Anyway, at this precise moment, the good pastor has parked his long black Cadillac at the bottom of the gated rise next to the Writer's shiny white El Camino and is trudging up the drive toward the house. He pauses every few steps to, I'm sorry to say, squeeze his crotch at the recollection of certain images he finds pleasing.

3. The corpse of Ephriam Crafter, embalmed and buried years ago, now rests flipped over in his coffin, the coffin lid up, and the rather rudely opened grave-plot sits there on the side of the house for all the world to see.

4. The nefarious quadruplets known as the Larkins Boys— men in their mid-forties but they're still thought of as "boys"—have suffered a devastating loss in that one of their numbers, namely the brother known as Horace, has been murdered—nay—*mutilated* in a manner

hitherto never witnessed, nor ever even conceived by any member of the Larkins family (which is saying something). If the modus of Horace's demise can even be properly detailed, one would have to say that his considerable abdominal region has been *exploded* from the inside-out. In addition, his genitals were, not cut, but *yanked* entirely from his groin and left hanging on a tree, a macabre calling card. Tucker believes this to be the work of a local drug gang, while Gut—the most naive of the quadruplets—suspects the mythic local monster known as the Bighead. Since the grim discovery of Horace's body, Tucker has embarked in a westerly direction, while Gut and Clyde head easterly, all in search of clues that may lead them to the killer of their beloved brother, and we will see and hear no more of them until the *next* sequel.

And now, as M.R. James would say, we return to the historic present.

The Writer and Case had installed themselves in Crafter's basement with the intention of studying the situation further and making deductions as to what to do next. On a mid-19th century kneehole table that Crafter had used as a study platform, Page 238 of the stolen Voynich manuscript lay immediately next to the Writer's Samsung phone, whose LED screen now displayed the snapshot he'd taken of the drawing on Crafter's back. If anything, the crude depiction of the horned devil stood out in greater detail. But how could this be? And the Hell-born penis—when the Writer looked at it for some seconds—seemed to throb, and this throbbing actually seemed to *move* the green tube connected to it. The Writer winced, turned away, and rubbed his eyes.

He was about to make comment but then Case, who was looking at the manuscript page—was rubbing his own eyes. "Something about this Voynich stuff," Case said. "Look at it long enough, it plays tricks with your vision."

"I just got some of that too," said the Writer. "And I could've sworn five out of the six doorways were open, and belching flame."

"*They were,*" Case said emphatically, but when he looked at the snapshot now he saw that this was not so. All of the wood-plank doors in the drawing were closed, just like the originals were now, mere feet away from them. "Well, I'll be damned…"

Excellent choice of words. The Writer scratched his beard. "Are these pictures trying to tell us something?"

"Yeah," Case chuckled. "They're telling us to open the doors."

"To open the doors to *Hell,* you mean?"

"Evidently."

"And you think we should?"

Case didn't answer directly. "I think all things happen for a reason, and I think *we* are here for a reason. I believe that *God* put us here for a reason—ah, I can see you don't believe that."

The Writer's brow had popped. "I don't necessarily *dis*believe it. Since I've arrived in Luntville, I find I'm believing things wholeheartedly that I would've scoffed at days ago." As he'd said that, he recalled the image of the *empty* embalming table at Dawn's funeral parlor, which he'd previously seen very occupied by the immense corpse of the Bighead. "Okay," he conceded. "I'll buy it. God Himself put us here for a reason, so now I suppose that reason can only be that He wants us to open those doors, correct?"

"Oh, I doubt that," Case said. "Not the God who said 'Thou Shalt Not Kill.'" He smiled a blinding white smile. "We'd have to *sacrifice* a human being to do that. We'd have to *impale* someone through the heart on one of the door spikes."

The Writer paused for thought. "Hmm, yes, there is that. But isn't it likely that a lot of this intensive occult protocol from the Middle Ages is dressed up for the sake of ritualism?"

"Dressed up?"

"You know. Tinsel. Window decor, in the figurative sense. It's not really function, it's just there for looks. I'm sure a lot of the occult scriveners and heretical leaders exaggerated details for effect. Extra icing on the satanic cake."

"I guess I follow you," Case said. "And I suppose that sort of thing *did* go on during text translations, just like it did in the abbeys when all those monks were transcribing Holy Bibles. But...what's your point?"

"Maybe somebody simply made up the tephramancy business because it's sinister, burning hearts of sacrifants to ashes, etc." This notion was about as Left Field as anything that had ever occurred to the Writer, but it seemed to materialize in his head by its own choosing. "Maybe all that's actually called for is a simple blood offering. Blood offerings go back thousands of years before Christ."

Case seemed to be losing belief in the Writer's credulity. "What makes you think this?"

The Writer shrugged. "Well, I read it in an M.R. James story once."

Case's face creased up. "*Who?*"

The Writer opened his mouth to reply, paused, thought better of it, and said, "Doesn't matter. Here, let me try something." Opening a drawer on the knee-hole table, he fished around amongst semi-precious gemstones, satanic pendants, and other like items, and picked up a jeweled bodkin, or what Shakespeare called a dagger in *Hamlet*. Then, for the first time in his excessively prudent life he did something howlingly *im*prudent.

He poked—with more than a little force—the bodkin's point into the pad of his thumb.

"Oww! Fuck!" he yelled. "That hurt like a *motherfucker!*"

Case stared, blank-faced. "What, uh, what did you expect? Say, man, are you, by chance, drunk?"

"No, but I hope to be later." Blood welled quickly on his thumb, some dribbling on the floor. "I didn't think a little jab like that would hurt *that fucking much!*"

More big drops of blood dribbled off his thumb and spotted the floor. He rushed to the farthest wood-plank door on the left and immediately daubed blood onto the iron spike jutting from the center plank. *Yuck,* he thought. For such a minuscule puncture, it bled quite a bit. Eventually the thumb went into his mouth till the bleeding stopped. He didn't know what he liked least: the sight of blood or the rusty taste of it.

"Looks like your gig didn't work," Case said, indicating the still-closed doorways.

"It might take a while, you know?" the Writer offered. And then he turned—

—and screamed.

With no warning, a figure stepped out of the staircase. The Writer's heart stopped for a few beats, and even Case was caught by surprise, yelled, and shakily drew his pistol.

The newcomer chuckled and haphazardly raised his hands. "Don't shoot me. I'm only an evangelist."

Of course, it was Pastor Tommy Ignatius.

"Wow, Tommy," Case said with a laugh. "You scared the—"

"—the living *fuck* out of us," the Writer finished. His heart was thunking in his chest.

"Oh, sir, my good sir. Profane speech serveth *not* the Lord, and only isolates those who believe in Him."

"My apologies, pastor," the Writer returned, all the while thinking, *Just profane speech? What about profane deeds, like watching kiddie porn? And we mustn't forget the gummy worms...*

The "pastor" nodded to both men, then looked down at the phone and the vellum sheet on the knee-hole table. "Ah, yes, men, the devil's work here indeed." Then he looked around the entire basement. "And this must be the lair of the long-dead local warlock I've heard so much about. A fitting chamber for one who dances with the Enemy, eh? *Fugae Satanae.*"

The Writer winced at the man's inept attempt at Old Latin. "Yes, in fact you must've seen him on your way in."

"We, uh, we can explain the opened grave and coffin out front," Case said without a whole lot of conviction. "It just might...take a while."

"Ah, and what an explanation that should be," said Pastor Tommy with a southern-twang chuckle. "But I presume your infamous blasphemer was never actually buried at all..."

The Writer's face lengthened. "What?"

"The corpse in the coffin outside was Crafter," Case told him with a cocked brow.

The pastor idly thumbed the lapels on his plaid jacket with patches on the elbows, narrowing his eyes at both men. "Gentlemen, I hate to beg to differ, but when I came up the hill to the house I couldn't help but notice the opened grave and the opened casket. But you can take my word for it. The casket was empty."

The Writer and Case both turned their heads very slowly and looked at each other...

"Not good," the Writer croaked.

"It's got to be a mistake," Case said. "We both saw his corpse..."

And now, in another unorthodox and probably aggravating narrative stasis, I must ask the reader to modulate his or her perspective of the story and attempt to envision the basement and its current occupants in a "P.O.V." manner. Please pretend that your mind's eye is now a movie camera, in a film by the likes of a Hitchcock or a Polanski or an Ingmar Bergman. I reiterate: your eye is a camera, and now the camera is mounted on the ceiling, looking down...

We see the tops of the heads of the three men: Pastor Tommy by the table, and Case and the Writer a bit more to the right, all turned towards one another. Conversation amongst them is ensuing, but we can't hear what they're saying, we hear only half-muted chatter that seems echoic and sped up like a tape on fast-forward. In fact, even the movements of the three men seem sped up a little.

Now, if you will, recall the famous scene in Hitchcock's *Psycho* where a very suspicious Martin Balsam enters the Bates mansion. The camera, like your mind's eye, is mounted on the ceiling, looking down, and we see Mr. Balsam—I should say, the top of Mr. Balsam's head—at the top of the stairs, and just as he sets foot on the landing, we also see the top of the head of an indiscernible person dart out of a room on the right, attack Mr. Balsam with a knife, then just as swiftly retreat back into the room. It's one of the most effective and terrifying scenes ever filmed; it even tops the "Shower" scene.

Anyway, all that aside, something quite similar in perspective and content is about to happen here in Ephriam Crafter's very occultishly appointed basement.

This is what we see:

Remember now, the "camera" is pointing down from the ceiling. We hear rapid footfalls, like a tape sped up, the footfalls of someone coming very quickly and deliberately down the stairs, and it is then that we see the top of the head of an indiscernible person emerge from the bottom of the stairwell. The heads of the Writer and Case and Pastor Tommy begin to turn toward this sound, and then we hear more fast-forward half-muted chatter.

Watch carefully, now.

The figure belonging to the top of the head of our new intruder slams hard into the Writer, who collapses and exclaims in squeaky fast-forward speech something like "Fuck! I'm too fat and old for this shit!" and next the intruder darts toward Case who is in the process of bearing his pistol around but the pistol is slapped out of his hand and then he is knocked to the floor by the forearm of our intruder, who then turns to the one person in the room who remains standing: Pastor Tommy Ignatius.

We can't see it from the downward angle, but you can take my word that the good pastor is blubbering in panic, stepping feebly back with his hands out, pissing and shitting his freshly ironed blue jeans, and jabbering incoherent prayers to a God who was likely too pissed off at him to give a shit.

We see, looking down, the indistinct shape of the intruder grab Pastor Tommy by the shoulders of his elbow-patched jacket, then slam his back against the wooden-planked door on the far left, impaling him through the heart on the door's iron spike. No more gummy worms in the dick for *this* holy man!

The wood-plank door to the farthest right swooshes open. The intruder, in an appropriate gesture of celebration, raises his hands over his head, bows forward, and then darts into the open doorway, after which he is seen no more.

Now we return to the normal perspective we expect in competent third-person fiction.

"Holy *fuck*," the Writer groaned, dragging himself back to his feet. When he inadvertently looked at the last door on the left and Pastor Tommy dead and skewered on the spike, he said it again. "Holy *fuck!*"

"Yeah, holy fuck is right!" Case exclaimed. He picked up his pistol and sprang to his feet. "Did you *see* that? Please tell me you saw what just happened!"

The Writer stared emptily "I...someone came down the stairs

and knocked me down. I didn't see who. Did you?"

"Yeah! It was Ephriam Crafter!"

This information jolted the Writer but of course the reader had already guessed that. "You mean, you mean…the *corpse* of Ephriam Crafter—"

"*Yeah!*"

"Crafter's reanimated corpse, a—a zombie—"

"Yeah! Tommy wasn't lying when he said the coffin was empty! Crafter ran down here, slammed Tommy against the spike, and then *opened the bridle!*"

When Case pointed to the opened door at the far right, the Writer almost collapsed.

Strangely, where one might rightly expect a cacodemoniacal blare, no sound came from the black doorway, and there were no flames as depicted in the illustration on Crafter's back.

Case stuffed his pistol in his belt and stepped forward. "You're with me, right?"

The Writer's face creased. "*Pardon me?*"

"I'm going in. Aren't you coming too?"

The Writer made a hacking sound in his throat. "Am I— No! I'm not going in there! *Hell* is on the other side of that door! Are you nuts?"

Case shrugged. "God will protect me. And it's my destiny. God *wants* me to do this; otherwise, why would He have brought me here?"

"Look, man. I guarantee you, God does *not* want you to go to Hell."

"Why not? It's not like I won't come back." Case seemed ecstatic at the possibilities. "I'm a Christian soldier. Imagine the good I can do for the Church—"

The Writer's eyes bugged. "By walking through a door to Hell?"

"Sure. I'm gonna look around, snap some pix with my cell, then come back and tell the world. When people hear my account and see the pix to go along with it? The number of the world's believers will *double!*"

He's insane, thought the Writer.

"Besides, I wanna see where Crafter went. Don't you?"

"No!"

Case winked. "And with any luck, I'll find the Devil and kick his ass!"

The Writer knew now there was no changing Case's mind. "If you go through that doorway, I don't think you'll ever come back out."

"Relax! I *know* I'll get back. I'm psychic, remember? I've foreseen it." And then Case nodded, grinned, and sprinted into the doorway.

Oh, for dick's sake. What is wrong with people? And what am I supposed to do now?

He felt brainless when he thunked up the stairs. The first logical thing to do, he supposed, was find the girls and tell them what happened, or—strike that.

The first logical thing to do was get a beer, which he retrieved from the cooler and, without Dawn's teeth to avail themselves as an opener, he found an opener in the kitchen. *Better,* he thought after a sip, but...how much better could things really be with a doorway to Hell standing wide open downstairs, not to mention the impaled corpse of an evangelical minister?

He shrugged, then started down the hall in search of Snowie and Dawn. Not long into his quest, he heard a shower running in one of the bedrooms, and he frowned. *It doesn't take THAT LONG to take a shower! Women! We've got a door to Hell open downstairs and these two floozies have been in there fisting each other for the last half hour!* but as he took one angry stride toward the door, he heard movement behind him, and a voice:

"Hey, here we are!"

The Writer turned to espy none other than Snowie and Dawn, wet-haired and now fully dressed, in the entry to the front parlor. "We found the washer and dryer so we cleaned our clothes, then we took showers," Dawn informed him.

"Yeah," Snowie said, "warshed all that yucky demonic puke off a us."

The Writer paused. "Ah, of course." He pointed to the bedroom door. "But I guess you're not much into water conservation, because you left the shower running."

"Huh?" Snowie said, head atilt.

"We took our showers in the bedroom in the next wing," Dawn said with a weird look in her eye.

Naturally, the question which next begged to be asked, the Writer asked himself: *If Snowie and Dawn are standing right here, then WHO THE FUCK is in there taking a shower?*

Lord knew he'd had enough surprises today—none of them particularly pleasant—yet with very little hesitation, he walked into this closest bedroom. One door inside was opened an inch, and it was from here that the unmistakable sound of the shower issued.

Just as he pushed the door open, the shower squeaked off, and then a muted rustle was heard, as of someone drying off with a towel.

When the door had opened fully, the Writer could only stare.

A rather wild looking nude woman had just alighted from the shower. Describing her with any accuracy of detail will take more words than any writer cares to expend; I'll only say that she was *peculiarly* attractive, about 5'6", well-breasted, and shapely. Very little body fat was in evidence; hard, toned muscles moved beneath tight skin, though they were not body-builder muscles, but instead the muscles of hard work for a very protracted period of time. The woman's hair provided her most arresting feature: it was a dark brown, like bittersweet chocolate, and since it had just been washed and wrung out, it hung down her back like a stout rope, and this "rope" extended just past her knees. Clearly, it hadn't been cut in decades, and the same, too, for her pubic hair: a veritable clump of unruly black hair, and smaller clumps spouted at her underarms.

When she looked up in surprise, the Writer got his first glimpse of her face: not stunning but not unattractive. A plain face, just touched by age-lines and some crow's feet. The Writer guessed her to be in her early-to mid-forties. And, of course, the Sexist Slob in the Writer had no choice but to make an especial survey of her breasts: they were "ample," they were "MILF-boobs," big but with just a touch of sag, as one might find on a woman who rarely wore bras. Dark, big, papillated nipples—if, indeed, "papillated" was a real word. When she stood upright, the Writer took greater note of her absolutely flat, fatless abdomen as well as the modest "six-pack." On each side were some faint stretch-marks, indicating she'd given birth at one time.

But here description ceased and the climax advances.

"Oh, hi," she said, startled. She covered herself haphazardly. "I'm sorry, but your front door was standing open. I came in and called out but no one answered. Anyway, I took the liberty of using your shower. I hope you don't mind."

The Writer replied in a spacy drone. "It's not my house, but...the owner won't mind. He's...indisposed at the moment."

She continued drying herself nonchalantly. "Believe it or not, that's the first shower I've had in, I guess, about twenty years."

"*What!*"

"Yep. Until just now, it's been lakes and streams, the Boone River, things like that." She smiled. "And let me tell you, that's no fun in the winter!"

Am I dreaming? the Writer wondered with some aggravation. This situation was absurd but then so was everything else about today. *Crafter came back to life. He sacrificed Tommy Ignatius and opened a traversion bridle to Hell. A psychic black guy named Case followed him into it, and on top of all that, my own doppelganger let the Bighead escape last night.*

Yes. What more absurdity could there be?

Plenty more.

"Oh, by the way, my name's Charity Wells." She wrapped the towel snugly around herself. "I 'went off the radar' as they say, a long time ago. But now I've come back to the real world."

The Writer squinted. "Okay, that's great, Charity. But why are you here, in this house, right now—I mean, besides to take a shower?"

She turned and bent over, wringing out her thick rope of hair some more over the shower drain. "That's difficult to answer, and if I answered you honestly, you wouldn't believe me."

At this, despite the pervading strangeness and seriousness of the situation, the Writer laughed out loud. "Charity, please, try me."

"Okay, you asked for it. Have you ever heard a local legend about a monster called the Bighead?" She turned back around and looked right at him.

He stared back, and in a response more like a dry gulp, said, "Yes."

She smiled and shrugged. "I'm the Bighead's twin sister."

TO BE CONTINUED...

ABOUT THE AUTHOR

Edward Lee has authored close to 50 books in the field of horror; he specializes in hardcore fare. His most recent novels are THE DOLL HOUSE and WHITE TRASH GOTHIC. His movie HEADER was released on DVD by Synapse Film in June, 2009. Lee lives in Largo, Florida.